Alpha Book Publisher

Alpha Book Publisher
www.alphapublisher.com
ISBN: 978-1-954297-50-0

Ordering Information:
Quantity sales. Special discounts are available on quantity purchases by corporations, associations, and others. For details, contact the publisher at the address above.
Orders by U.S. trade bookstores and wholesalers. Visit www.alphapublisher.com/contact-us to learn more.

Printed in the United States of America

Alpha Book Publisher

Alpha Book Publisher

I would like to dedicate this book to my Mother Lois Foutch who was always there for me and had faith in me. She gave me love, support, and encouragement.

Alpha Book Publisher

Table of Contents

Alpha Book Publisher

Alpha Book Publisher

CITY OF CHAOS

AND

MAYHEM

BY

ELIZABETH FOUTCH

Alpha Book Publisher

CHAPTER 1

As I lie awake in bed at 2 a.m., I hear the sounds of sirens going by in the distance. The rain is coming down hard, thundering and lightning the sirens are getting closer and closer. I hear a lot of screaming and shouting from my neighbor's Lucy and Jimmy and gunshots or could be a car backfiring, it's hard to tell.

I got out of bed and went to the window to see what all the commotion was but it's so dark and the visibility is terrible that I couldn't see much through the fog and heavy rain.

I'm Shiloh and I'm a retired Navy veteran. I live in St Louis in a three-story Brick House. The third floor has three bedrooms and a full bath with beautiful red plush carpet throughout and a roof you can walk out on which is where I like to sunbathe. On the second floor, there's a nice big family room where I have my pool table with a Budweiser sign hanging overhead, and in the living room a beautiful crystal chandelier is hanging from the ceiling, there's two bedrooms, a full bath all with hardwood floors. A balcony overlooks the front and a balcony overlooks the back alley… The first floor is where my uncle Vito lives. Uncle Vito is from Brooklyn, New York, he has always been in and out of trouble since he was 10. At age 17 he was sentenced to prison for robbing a liquor store and killing the clerk. Vito is 5'11" with Sandy brown hair and 320 lbs. He spends a lot of time at the race track gambling and at the bars drinking. He owns Vito's boxing gym in downtown St. Louis and is always looking to score; whether it's money, drugs, weapons, or women. He has quite the reputation with the ladies.

Mom comes running into the living room yelling "Take cover Shiloh I got my rifle" as she pokes the barrel out the window.

Put the rifle down and go back to bed. We are not under attack.

"Fine!" Mom disappears into the other room.

I looked out the window and I saw a figure running across the street. I went into Mom's room and she's gone. The doorbell rings and as I go running down the stairs, I missed the bottom step and fell on my face.

"Who is it?" I shouted through the door.

"It's Detective Lorenzo."

I cracked the door and he shows me his badge. Detective Lorenzo is Puerto Rican and 5' 8" with black hair and a well-trimmed beard and mustache with green eyes, very handsome.

"What can I do for you, detective? It's 2:30 in the morning, can this wait?"

"No ma'am. There's a fugitive on the loose in the area, I'm letting everyone know to be on the lookout and keep your doors locked, he's armed and dangerous."

He shows me a picture of a man in his mid-forties with long black hair pulled back in a ponytail with dark eyes and a scar from his eye down his cheek. He goes by the name of Mad Dog.

"Yes detective thank you I will let you know if I hear or see anything." He hands me his card. I looked across the street and saw a shadow again but I could barely make it out.

Oh my God, it's Mom all dressed in black with her pistol and she's running across the street like a crazy person. She's been watching too many of those Ninja movies.

What in the hell are you doing?

I'm on the lookout. I've got a bad feeling

something bad is going to happen. I’m here to make sure it doesn't. No time to talk Shiloh, I'll be on the roof if you need me. Don't worry, everything's going to be okay.

Don't worry she says! How can I not worry with my crazy ass mom thinking she is a Ninja with a gun and running around the neighborhood. It’s a wonder my hair is not snow white by now.

Mom is 71 years old 5’ 2”, 125 lbs feisty as hell, with gray spiked hair and purple highlights. She dresses like she's in her twenties with her Spandex and high heel Fringe boots and a low-cut blouse showing too much cleavage with her 44DD about to pop out.

I don't think that’s necessary so why don't you come back in the house and get some rest.

Okay, I’ll be right down, as she slides down the drain pipe her heel gets stuck and she flips upside down, the pipe breaks and both her and the pipe come tumbling down.

Ouch that hurt, oh shit I peed on myself.

None of that would have happened if you would have listened to me in the first place. You're always getting into a pickle.

No, I don't want a pickle honey, I'm not hungry, but thanks for asking.

I didn't ask if you wanted a pickle. Just come inside. Do you need me to help you? Are you hurt?

No, I'm not hurt, just my pride. I think I've got it and I will take that pickle now and a beer. Lord knows I need one. Hey, I got a big fat doobie, you want to smoke it with me?

No, I don't think so. I'm going to bed and I think you need to also Mom.

I'm going to stay up for a while and play some pool, drink, and smoke some weed and keep an eye on things. I have Cochise and Nikita here to help me if the need arises.

Cochise and Nikita are Shiloh's two German Shepherds. Nikita is a white female who loves everyone and Cochise is a male and sable in color he is the enforcer.

Okay mom, good night, see you in the morning. Cochise, you keep an eye on her for me. He turns his head from side to side as if to say REALLY!!!

Cochise and Nikita both love mom so much and always look out for her. They also love to help her out whenever possible. The Three Musketeers. They sure know how to cause trouble and there's definitely never a dull moment with the three of them around.

Yep, I think I should keep on dying my hair. Those three will be the death of me yet.

Good night dear and don't worry about a thing.

So comforting to know.

Two days ago, I received a phone call from a man I served with in the Navy, his name is Ace, he is 6'2" muscular with black hair and gorgeous baby blue eyes. He captured my heart the moment I laid my eyes on him. We dated for a bit but lost contact when I had to come back to St Louis because my mom needed me. 10 years later I received a phone call from him saying he needs to talk to me and that it's urgent. We set up a meeting for 10 a.m. the next morning at L & B bar right around the corner from where I live on Spring and Wyoming.

CHAPTER 2

It's 5 a.m. and Vito is banging on the ceiling yelling at me to come down and get my crazy ass drunk mother. Mom and Vito hate each other, mom was married to Vito's brother and he is convinced that mom killed his brother and had gotten away with it. Mom had gotten $250,000 from Dad's life insurance and she opened her nightclub on the East side called Katz Bar and Grill.

Okay Vito, I'm on my way, as I go running down the back stairs to his apartment, I hear Vito and Mom yelling at each other.

Why are you down here bothering Uncle Vito?

I heard a noise, so I had to check it out.

She was hiding in my closet and thought she was invisible. Duke sniffed her out when she started passing gas and stinking up the place. (Duke is Vito's big black ferocious Doberman Pinscher). He scared the crap out of your mom so she pissed all over my closet and tried to use her pepper spray on him and when I grabbed her out she tried to use her stun gun on me. Then when none of that worked, she had the nerve to try to seduce me.

I'm really sorry Uncle Vito. Okay mom we need to go now. Mom is drunker than a skunk but a smooth operator. I'm trying to lead her upstairs but she is staggering all over the place.

I'm fine Shiloh, I managed to do what I had to.

What have you gone and done now mom?

You don't need to worry about it Shiloh, I'm going to bed now.

That's the best idea I've heard yet.

It's 10:00 a.m. and the phone is ringing. I answered the phone and it's Ginger. She is mom's partner and best friend and they run Katz together. Ginger is 70 years old, 130 lbs. and dresses like she is in her 20's also. Her hair is grey with red highlights. What a pair these two are, trouble follows them everywhere they go.

Mom, Ginger's on the phone.

"Did you take care of the old fart?" Ginger asks.

Yes, I managed to bug his house. He was there and had no clue, I'll tell you about it when you get here.

I'm on my way. Dillan has more surveillance equipment if we need it.

We can go back when everyone is gone and get the evidence we need to take him down. I can borrow Dillan's surveillance equipment. He has all kinds of gadgets we can use. I'll be over in an hour. Dillan is Ginger's off-and-on boyfriend and is a retired police chief. He is 66 years old, 185 lbs., with reddish-brown hair and green eyes.

Kitty (mom) is taking the trash out to the alley and smells something horrible near the dumpster, she opens the dumpster and starts screaming and yelling for someone to call the police. All the neighbors come running out to see what all the fuss was about.

Kitty starts pointing to the dumpster with a horrified look on her face and all she could get out of her mouth was Body.

The police arrive and right behind them come the ambulance and fire trucks. The coroner arrives shortly after to pronounce the man dead and takes him away. No one knows who this man is or what had happened.

CHAPTER 3

When Ginger finally arrived, she was wearing her denim skirt with red leggings, heels, and a denim jacket with a blue silk blouse chewing her gum like Flo in the TV series Alice.

What's with all the cops? Did they finally arrest Vito?

No, I found a dead body in the dumpster when I was taking out the trash.

Damn, why do I always have to miss all the action? Does anyone know who it is?

Maybe it's one of Vito's victims.

No one knows who he is or what has happened. I need a joint and a drink. I'm too old for all this shit.

Okay let's go behind the house to smoke a doobie and I'll buy you a drink over at L & B, then we can also discuss how we're going to get that S.O.B. Vito.

Ginger is at the bar ordering drinks and Kitty is at the jukebox when a man walks up behind her and smacks her ass and says, "I've been looking all over for you."

Well, congratulations you found me.

That's no way to treat an old friend now is it? He grabs her and kisses her then punches in a song on the jukebox taking her by the hand and starts dancing to the sound of "When a man loves a woman" by Percy Sledge.

Ginger brings over a couple of beers for her and Kitty and sets them down on the table then goes to the dance floor and smacks Tiny on the ass and says, "hey sexy where have you been?" Come and have a drink with us.

Tiny is 6'8" brown hair, hazel eyes, and 220 lbs. he has always been in love with Kitty but something has always gotten in the way. Tiny is an ex-Marine in his mid-60's and still runs 5 miles a day. He is retired now and has come looking for Kitty to try and win her over.

Ginger is a big flirt, she plays stroking on the jukebox and starts to give Tiny a lap dance. Ginger says to Tiny, "When are you going to take me for a spin in that convertible of yours?"

"How about now we can all go for a spin and you can show me Katz club, I haven't been there and would love to see it."

"Well let's rock and roll then."

Friday night at Katz on the east side is always poppin. We walk into Katz and its wall-to-wall people. Fiona is up on-stage dancing. She is everyone's favorite. Fiona is a sweet Mexican girl 23 years old with long brown hair and 120 lbs., she is trying to put herself through school so she can be a makeup artist in California for all the rich and famous people. The place is filled with smoke from all the smokers. We walk into another room and there's a pool tournament going on and a few people playing darts.

We go outside and people are smoking, drinking, and dancing and enjoying themselves.

Tiny says, "looks like you ladies have done really well for yourselves."

"Yes, we have, going on eight years now."

Shiloh walks in and sees Tiny right away and goes up to him and gives him a big hug and kiss on the cheek. I haven't seen you in forever, I'm so glad to see you. What brings you to these parts?

I came to find your mom, I've been thinking a lot about her lately and something was telling me to come to see her. Is she okay?

You know mom always into something. She

and uncle Vito at each other's throats again, then she finds a dead body in the dumpster behind our house and no one knows who he is or what had happened. She was pretty shaken up over that.

Wow! I had no idea, that's terrible, she hasn't said anything about that to me.

She probably won't either.

Boy, you sure have grown up since the last time I've seen you. You are such a beautiful young woman. Do you have a man in your life? I bet you have lots of men after you.

Thanks, but no I don't and I'm not really looking either. I don't have time right now anyway. Well, I better go find mom and see what she is up to, it was so nice seeing you Tiny. You should stop by sometime for dinner.

Yes, I will definitely have to.

Oh my god, mom! What are you doing? Get off that pole before you break something. Fiona doesn't need any pointers from you, she is doing just fine. What has gotten into you lately?

"I am so sorry honey," Shiloh says to Fiona.

It's okay Shiloh, she is only trying to be helpful.

Shiloh, sweetheart, what brings you here?

Just checking on you mom, especially since everything that has been going on lately.

I'm fine since Ginger came to get me. We smoked a couple of doobies and had a few drinks then Tiny met us at L & B bar and we went cruising around in his convertible.

I think I might rock his world later.

Mom, I don't think I need to be hearing this.

We hear this cheering all of a sudden so we go to check it out and it's Ginger up on the bar dancing so mom whistles real loud and everyone makes way for her and the crowd helps her up on the bar also, now both of them are on the bar dancing like a couple of young girls to the tune of the wooly bully.

Damn, your mom and Ginger have got some moves, not too shabby.

Tiny don't you get any wild ideas.

Too late, already done.

I look across the room and Detective Lorenzo is looking and smiling at me so I walk across the room to him.

Hi Detective, what brings you here?

I was in the neighborhood so I thought I would come in and check out the place and have a drink.

Looks like your mom and Ginger know how to party and have a good time. Do you take after your mom?

Yea, well my mom is a little wild and crazy. She never used to be like that until dad died, now she's like this whole other person I don't even know.

Give her a break. She is just having a little fun and living a little, there's no harm in that, is there? She's had a really hard life and your father didn't let her do much. Now she's free as a bird and enjoying life again.

Have you heard anything about who the body belonged to that was found in the alley detective?

They are doing an autopsy now so we won't know for a few days.

Do you have any news on the escaped man that you were on the hunt for?

We have a few leads but I can't really discuss that.

Well Shiloh it was nice seeing you but I have to leave now, I need to get started early in the morning.

Yes detective, and please let me know what you find out, good night.

CHAPTER 4

It's 8 a.m. and my alarm is going off, I have to get up and get ready for my meeting with Ace. I'm in the kitchen cooking eggs, hash browns, toast, and coffee when mom comes strolling in.

Mom! Are you just now getting home?

Yes, we had a long night and I'm tired and hungry.

Well, have some breakfast then go get some rest. I have to go meet Ace. Do you need me to go with you?

No, I'll be fine but thank you, just get some rest.

It's 95 degrees outside so I throw on my blue sundress with my white sandals; my long black hair is in a bun under my white hat with my sunglasses on. I walk next door for my meeting with Ace.

Ace is sitting at a small rustic hand-carved table with soft black leather cushions in the back corner where it is quiet so we can talk. He has a cup of freshly brewed coffee waiting for me when I walk in. The smell is lightly caramelized and almost nutty, the aroma files the whole place with a sensational smell.

He is wearing a red muscle shirt with a pair of white shorts and a pair of black sandals. His muscles and his arms and legs are bulging among other things and you can tell he still works out faithfully.

He sees me walk in and stands to give me a hug and kiss, pulls out my chair for me to sit down then he takes his seat.

It's so good to see you Shiloh, how have you been? Can I get you anything?

I'm doing good Ace. Wow, it's been a long time, you look great. So, what is so urgent that you need to speak to me about?

I'm afraid I have some bad and disturbing news baby, remember when we were in the Military and you arrested Captain Steward for rape and he was court marshaled and was sentenced to prison?

Yes, I remember it like it was yesterday.

Well, he's been in and out of prison since then but this last time he escaped killing two police officers.

Okay, so what does this have to do with me?

I'm telling you this because when his cell was being searched, they found some pictures of you and your family and a diary with entries saying how you were going to pay for ruining his life and you had to be taught a lesson.

You wouldn't even notice him now. He's a really dangerous man and goes by a different name now. He knows where you live and everything about you. He goes by the name of Mad Dog.

Why Mad Dog? Is it because he is mad all the time? She laughs.

I'm being serious Shiloh, this is no laughing matter.

Your life is at risk now.

Okay, I'm sorry.

I have a picture of him. (He pulls out a picture and puts it on the table for Shiloh to see.

Oh my God!! This is the guy from the other night. There was a police chase and he got away. A detective came to my door and said to be on the lookout for him. He must have known the guy was coming for me and didn't even tell me. I will be giving Detective Lorenzo a call.

Well, I'm not leaving you to take him on by yourself. We made a great team back in the day.

After all these years and you're still looking out for me, thank you. (kisses him on the cheek.)

I still love you Shiloh, always have and always

will. I don't know what I would do if anything happened to you. It was unfortunate that you had to split when you did but I understand you had to come back and take care of your mom.

How is your mom doing?

She is always into something, just wait till you meet her. She lives with me.

I can't wait to meet the little lady. (He smiles; his smile just melts my heart.)

I have an extra room I will fix up for you.

You mean I won't be sharing your room? (He says playfully.)

How about I buy you lunch and we can catch up and maybe have a few drinks like back in the day

That sounds great. Let's just grab something quick from Naugles then we can go across the river to Katz and have a few drinks and talk. Mom bought Katz after dad died. It's a bar and grill with a few dancers and is a really nice place, she is doing really good business despite her craziness. Maybe that's why everyone loves her so much. (She laughs.)

"She sounds like she's a lot of fun."

"If that's what you want to call it." (She laughs.)

"Well, we can just eat at Katz then and I can try

out the food there."

"Okay, sounds good but I must warn you it gets pretty crazy on the weekends."

"It's all good the crazier the better."

"Okay, but remember I warned you."

Saturday night at Katz is always poppin. It's wall to wall people as usual and standing room only. Pool tournaments and dart tournaments going on in the other room, poker games going on in the back room, people are dancing on two different dance floors, outside in the enclosed area everyone is smoking, drinking, and dancing, rappin (talking), and falling down drunk and in the back corner there is a big fight going on.

Mom runs out with her pistol and starts yelling for them to stop and starts shooting in the air.

"Stop that damn fighting now or I'll blow a hole in your knee caps and you'll end up in a damn wheelchair."

Big Al comes running out to take care of the situation. Big Al is 450 lbs., black with dreads and a gold tooth in front, and looks like a sumo wrestler. He wrestles one guy to the ground and another guy rolls up behind him and stabs him in the side, blood starts to ooze out everywhere.

Mom runs over and shoots the guy in the kneecap.

"I told you all to stop your damn fighting in my club. Now get the hell out before I shoot the other knee and don't ever show your face around here again. Now any of you other hoodlums here want to try me?"

"Damn Miss Kitty you don't need me around here, you got this you're one bad ass mamma."

"We need to get you looked at Al. I'm taking you to the ER."

"The hell you are!!! Do you realize they are required to call the cops? We don't need any damn cops coming around here and snooping that's bad for business. I can patch myself up. I'll be okay it's only a flesh wound."

Big Al looks around and says "Now what's all the commotion about?"

A voice yells out. ("It's Fiona! Come quick!") Mom takes off with her .45 caliber in her hand.

A big burly man had grabbed Fiona and started touching her and kissing her.

In walks Shiloh and Ace. Ace sees what's

going on and walks up to the guy and just starts whaling on him and kicking his ass all the way outside and they are still fighting in the street. The big guy bites Ace in the leg to try and get away.

"Ace stop before you kill him."

Kitty runs over to help and gets hit in the face. "Oh no you didn't!" I know my gun is in here somewhere. Here it is and she accidentally pulls the trigger and shoots a hole in her purse. Damn, I have to quit doing that.

"Keep that crazy trigger-happy old woman away from me."

Kitty aims her gun at him and shoots but misses and shoots out the streetlight instead.

The guy takes off running and Kitty tries to run after him but Ace grabs her up and holds her back.

"Woah tiger, I think he gets the picture."

Kitty is flopping her hands and legs like a fish out of water. "Let me go you big ape. Who the hell is this guy?"

"Mom I'd like you to meet the big ape."

"Ace is the name. Glad to finally meet you."

"I wish I could say the same now put me down."

"Ace will be staying with us for a while. I fixed up the guest room for him. We served in the Military together." (Shiloh didn't want to tell her mom the real reason that Ace was there and get her all excited and worked up.)

In walks Ginger with blood all over her and she falls to the ground. (Mom starts yelling and asking what happened, but Ginger is unresponsive.)" Someone call 911 hurry!!" (Moms crying. Ginger is her best friend and partner they do everything together.)

The ambulance arrives and takes Ginger away. Shiloh and Ace drive mom to the hospital. They had to do surgery on her and were able to save her but now she is in a coma and not sure when she will wake up or even know what happened to her. The doctor told mom that this was normal for someone with her injuries and not to worry.

Mom calls Dillan and tells him what has happened to Ginger, he rushes to the hospital to be with her.

Dillan demands to know what happened to her, but no one knows. Dillan stays by Ginger's side and won't leave.

Big Al closes the club for Kitty since she is in no shape to do it herself, she goes home and tries to process everything that has happened in the last week and tries to make sense of it.

Mom is feeding her 5 cats and talking to them about her day as if she was expecting a response. She is also taking care of Nikita and Cochise, Shiloh's two German Shepherds, she lets them go out so they can do their business then they come right back in. Shiloh works with both dogs every day and is training them.

Mom is getting ready to hop into bed when she hears the doorbell ring. Who the hell can be ringing my doorbell at 3 a.m.? She wasn't going to answer it but the dogs were going crazy and wouldn't stop barking. She stumbles down the stairs and loses her balance and almost falls but Nikita was there to help her so she wouldn't fall.

"Who is it?"

"It's Tiny open the door."

"Do you know what time it is?"

"Yes, time for you to open the damn door."

"Hold on a minute." Mom opens the door and Tiny falls in the door. He smells of booze and reeks of weed. You look like hell, come on in if you can manage to walk up the stairs because I'm sure as hell not going to carry you.

Tiny staggers up the stairs into mom's room and passes out on her bed. Mom takes off his shoes and pants and covers him up then she climbs into bed and falls asleep.

Mom jumps out of bed at 7:30 a.m. so she can get ready to go to the hospital and see Ginger. Tiny is still sleeping and snoring so she just lets him sleep and she gets dressed then calls for a cab. Mom had her license suspended and is no longer allowed to drive so she has to take public transportation, get a ride or walk everywhere.

Mom jumps into a cab and goes to incarnate word hospital. Ginger is still in ICU and unresponsive. Dillan has not left her side all night.

"Dillian, you look like hell, why don't you go get something to eat and take a shower and freshen up a little, I will stay with Ginger."

"Okay, but don't leave her side for anything in case she wakes up. I don't want her to be alone for a minute. I will be back in about two hours."

"She is in good hands Dillian, I'm not going to

leave her for a minute. Now go take care of yourself, you won't be any good to Ginger if you don't take care of yourself too." Mom sits down in a chair next to Ginger's bed and holds her hand and just starts to cry.

I promise you Ginger I will find whoever did this to you and make them pay. Mom starts talking to God and praying for Ginger's recovery.

All of a sudden Ginger shows a little movement. Mom runs out to the hall and starts calling for the nurse or doctor to come quickly.

"Get your lazy asses in here now." The doctor and nurses come running in and they take Ginger's vitals and check her pupils, and everything is looking good.

"Ginger, I'm nurse Evelyn can you tell me what year it is?"

"Yes, 1975."

"Good, now can you tell me how many fingers I'm holding up?"

The nurse held up two fingers.

"Three."

"Okay, who is the President of the United States."

"Ford."

"Okay, good, the doctor will be in shortly to run some tests."

CHAPTER 5

Shiloh decides to go for a drive in her 1964 mustang convertible, it's a beauty, black with red flames on the hood, 5 speed, spinners, and a great stereo system you can hear two blocks away. It's one badass car.

Cochise and Nikita go riding with Shiloh; they love to go bye-bye. As Shiloh is driving, she notices a black 1966 GT40 is following her so she starts whipping in and out of streets and alleys to try and lose them. She succeeded in losing them but not before she managed to get a partial license plate number. She stopped at the corner of Grand and Gravois to use a payphone to call Detective Lorenzo. He told me to stay put and is on his way. While I was waiting, I decided to go into White Castles to get a bite to eat and bought Cochise and Nikita a couple of White Castles also, we ate in the parking lot while waiting on the detective. As I was waiting, I saw this black car go by again, but I don't think he spotted me.

Detective Lorenzo shows up and takes my statement and calls in the license plate number that I gave him, but it just happens that the car was reported stolen so he put an APB out on it and to rest assured that he would find it.

Shiloh decides to take a drive down to the riverfront with her dogs since that is where she does her best thinking. As she is sitting under a tree and the dogs are running and playing this car drives by real slow and starts taking pictures of her but she can't make out what the person looks like.

My dogs and I drove across town to Uncle Vito's boxing gym. Nikita stayed in the car while Cochise and I went in to see Vito.

Uncle Vito's gym is a plain red brick building on a small lot surrounded by a chain-link fence. The entrance to the gym is through a long dark hallway then up a staircase with very dim lighting. There are a few heavy bags, jump ropes hanging from hooks, twin boxing rings, mirrors, and shelves of gloves and mitts. There is one large locker room for the men and one small locker room for the women with two small bathrooms for both men and women. The smell is enough to knock you out, it is a moist sweetness, spiced leather and Lysol, sweat, and must.

"Uncle Vito, I need your help."

"Sure, what's up?'

Shiloh proceeds to tell him she's being followed by a black 1966 GT40 and she gives him the partial plate number that she wrote down. "I need to know who is following me and why."

Vito says, "sure thing babe, I'll get my boys right on it."

"Thanks Uncle Vito."

Vito calls a meeting with his boys and informs them of the situation and tells them to take care of the problem. "I also want someone to follow my niece to make sure nothing happens to her."

I arrive home and notice that my door has been broken into, so I pull out my piece and walk slowly up the stairs. I don't see anyone, but Cochise takes off running down the hall. The intruder is still in the house. The guy runs to the back balcony and jumps onto the roof next door and Cochise is still on him and jumps also and keeps chasing him. The house was ransacked, they were looking for something obviously, but what?

Cochise came back carrying something in his mouth, as he got closer, I noticed it was a boot and there was blood everywhere. It was Cochise's blood he had been shot. I called the emergency number for the Vet and they are waiting for our arrival. I get down on my hands and knees and pray over him and ask God for his help. “Please, please don’t let anything happen to him.”

We arrived at the Vet’s office and they took him back immediately to have surgery to remove the bullet.

“There were a few complications in removing the bullet, but it was successful. He needs to stay overnight for observation, we want to make sure he recovers smoothly.”

“Okay, but I’m not leaving, I'm staying by his side.”

“As you wish ma’am, there is a cot that you can sleep on right next to him.”

“Thank you.”

I called detective Lorenzo from the Vet office and told him what happened.

Detective Lorenzo comes to the Vet office to check on me and Cochise.

“I need some answers and I need them now Detective. You’re not telling me something, now what is it? I need to know.”

“Okay Shiloh, I will meet you later on and tell

you what I can.

Let's talk over dinner. I'll meet you at Shoney's at 7:00 PM.

"Fine, I will see you then!"

I called the hospital to talk to Dillian to see how Ginger is doing.

"Ginger is doing a lot better. She is out of ICU and has been moved to a private room, but she doesn't remember anything that has happened. The doctor says that is normal for someone of her injuries and her memory will come back in bits and pieces."

"I'm so relieved she's out of ICU but I won't be able to come and see her today. I am staying at the Vet hospital overnight with Cochise. He was shot and had to have surgery, he is in recovery and resting and I don't want to leave him alone."

"How did he get shot? What happened?"

"It's a long story I will fill you in later."

Cochise is sleeping so I slipped out for a while to go meet detective Lorenzo.

I arrived at Shoney's at 6:55 p.m. and detective Lorenzo was already there and had a table. Lorenzo pulls my chair out for me and then has a seat. I ordered a Jalapeño burger with bacon and crispy fries with a Dr. Pepper and Lorenzo ordered the parmesan chicken with a coke.

"Okay, let's cut to the chase and tell me what's going on. Let's start with the dead body in the dumpster in my alley."

"He was a homeless man named Joe Gilbert. He was probably at the wrong place at the wrong time. He took a pretty hard hit to the head and ruptured his brain. It is still under investigation as to why."

"What about everything else? You didn't tell me the first day you came to my door that the man that escaped is coming after me. Didn't you think I had the right to know this?"

"I didn't want to alarm you until I knew for sure. I have my best men on it and we will find him. There's also an APB out on the black GT40 that keeps following you and we are dusting your house for fingerprints. We are doing all we can right now."

Shiloh stands up and takes $20 out of her purse to pay for dinner but detective Lorenzo says he will take care of it.

"Well thank you, detective, I must get back to the Vet hospital and check on Cochise."

"You will be hearing from me Shiloh as soon as I find anything else out."

Detective Lorenzo pays for dinner and goes back to the department to see if anything else has come up.

I get back to the Vet hospital and Cochise is still sleeping. Nikita is lying beside him; they are very close. I curl up on the cot and cover-up and fall asleep.

It's 7:00 a.m. and I get woken up by Cochise and Nikita. They have to go out and use the bathroom. Cochise is trying to act like he's better, but you can tell he is still sore from his wound.

The doctor gets there at 8:00 a.m. and examines Cochise and releases him to go home. He has been prescribed some antibiotic ointment and some pain medication and says he needs to try and rest for the next week.

"That's easier said than done but I will do my best."

I fixed up a crate for him so when I'm gone he can rest and not be bothered.

Nikita stays by his side; she just loves him so much.

It's Sunday evening and I'm sitting on the front balcony watching the neighborhood kids ride their big wheels, playing frisbee, jumping rope, playing hopscotch, skating, and hula hooping. It's always such a joy to watch all the children laughing and playing.

The streetlights start to come on and that's when the children know it's time to go home.

I gave Cochise his antibiotic ointment and pain medication and he's sound asleep now and resting. I go down on the front porch with my harmonica and one of Uncle Vito's boys is down there patrolling and guarding the house.

Macc is a big black guy 5'11" with a beard and 270 lbs., with 6 gold teeth. He was in prison with Vito on drug charges and recently just got out. Vito hired him as a bodyguard to watch over me.

"How's everything going tonight Miss Shiloh?"

"Living the dream Macc."

I start playing some blues on my harmonica and Ace hears me and grabs his guitar and joins me, Vito comes out with his saxophone and joins in. We all start playing Big Boss Man by Jimmy Reed.

It's getting late and a lot of traffic is starting to

come in and out of Vito's. It livens up around 11:00 p.m.

I stand up and point to the street and yell, "There's that car that's been following me."

Macc and Ace jump on their Harleys and go after him. Vito yells for them to bring him back alive.

The chase is on and the GT40 is trying to lose the bikes, whipping in and out of traffic and speeding down the alleys knocking over trash cans everywhere. Macc blocks the alley on one end and Ace races to the other end of the alley to block him. There's no place for him to go now so he jumps out of his car and runs through a yard to get to the street and out of nowhere here comes Kitty on her bike and cuts him off at the pass and shoots him in the kneecap and then runs into him on her bike. Ace and Macc pull up and say, "We got this Miss Kitty," Macc ties his hands together and ties him to the bike and he has to run behind the bike with blood pouring down his leg from where he was shot. Kitty is riding behind them to make sure he doesn't get away and she has a whip and keeps smacking his ass telling him to get a move on.

They arrive back at the house and tie him up in

the basement with chains and leave him there for a while, but Kitty is staying to keep an eye on him and she has her whip and gun. My life is never dull with mom around!!

Cochise goes down into the basement with mom and starts barking and growling at the guy. He was the one who shot Cochise, you can still see the teeth marks on his leg.

"Keep that crazy dog and maniac old lady away from me."

"You dumb shit you shot him and he almost died, you're lucky I don't let him loose on you."

Mom asks, "Who are you, who sent you, and why are you following my daughter?"

"I'm not telling you jack shit Bitch?"

"You will if you don't want a hole in your other knee cap."

"Go to Hell!!!"

Macc comes back down in the basement to see how mom is doing.

Macc tells mom to go get some air and he will take care of him and watch him until Vito gets there.

"Okay, but don't take your eyes off that polecat for one second."

"I won't Miss Kitty."

"Crazy old psychopath, she needs to be locked up."

Mom goes upstairs and has Tiny drive her to the local 905 store up on Grand, she needs a bottle of Hill and Hill, her favorite whiskey. As soon as they leave 905 mom tells Tiny she has the munchies, so they stop over at White Castles.

Tiny turns mom's head toward him and kisses her and tells her he loves her. We need to sit down and have a serious talk Kitty; you can't avoid it forever.

"I'm not avoiding it Tiny, I'm just not ready yet."

"It's been eight years since Vinny's death. It's time to move on with your life and I want to spend the rest of our lives together."

"I'm sorry Tiny I just can't make that kind of commitment right now. You know what my life was like when I was married to Vinny. I'm actually being able to enjoy my life now so let's just enjoy now and not try to rush the future."

"Well, I'm here to stay Kitty and I will wait because you are worth waiting for and I love you."

"Thank you. I just need more time." (She kisses

him on the cheek). "I think I'm just going to walk home and do some thinking; I'll catch up with you later."

Mom decides to walk home down Grand Avenue over to Grace Avenue by Rose Fanning school on over to Spring Avenue. It's such a beautiful night out, it's 92 degrees and the stars are shining bright and the moon is full. She is wearing her tight black leather pants with 4" heel fringe boots with a red silk low cut blouse showing plenty of cleavage.

A white van with two masked men pulls up beside mom and the two of them jump out and try to grab her but she is quick on her feet and pulls out her stun gun and gets one of them in his nuts and he is temporarily paralyzed. The other assailant tries to tackle her to the ground, but mom whacks him in the head with her purse and it's pretty heavy with everything she has in there. She takes out her pepper spray and sprays him in the eyes. They are both screaming on the ground trying to get it together. Mom takes off running down the street and makes it home before the two men could come after her.

Mom gets home and goes running upstairs and she's pissed. She changes into her camouflage clothes and puts her headband on and grabs her shotgun.

"What's going down baby? Where are you going dressed like that? Talk to me!!" Tiny says to her.

Mom gets on the phone and calls Ginger and tells her what happened.

"I'm on my way, I'll be there in five minutes."

Ginger got out of the hospital a few days ago, everything is still a little fuzzy, but she wanted to come home because she thought it might jog her memory better if she was at home in familiar surroundings.

Mom runs out and jumps on her Indian dirt bike. Ginger pulls up on her Indian and Tiny follows and jumps on his Harley. Shiloh calls detective Lorenzo and files him in. The white van is nowhere in sight and Kitty can't identify the men on account they were wearing ski masks. Shiloh goes down to the basement to find Macc.

"I need to talk to you Macc."

"What's good Miss Shiloh?"

"Nothing is good Macc, I need to hire you; I know you work for my uncle Vito, but I really need your help and I know you have all kinds of connections.

"Yeah! What do you need me to do Miss "S"?"

"Someone is trying to hurt my mom and I need to know who and why and what they are after."

"It won't be cheap Miss Shiloh."

"I don't care about the money; I just need results."

"Yes ma'am, I'm on it."

Mom, Ginger and Tiny return back to the house, the van is long gone.

Detective Lorenzo was waiting in the living room when they returned.

"I'm going to find those scumbags if it's the last thing I do and when I do, I'm going to shoot them in the kneecaps and cripple them. "

Lorenzo stands up as the three of them take the last stair.

"Detective Lorenzo is here to help and take your statement about what happened tonight," Shiloh tells mom.

"The good detective here has taken several statements over the last few weeks and has not produced any results for us so why in the hell would I want to give him a statement. Thanks, but no thanks, detective, I will handle this my way. They have messed with the wrong old lady this time, I've had it." (Mom turns and walks away.)

Tiny goes into the bathroom and runs Kitty a nice hot bubble bath and makes her a stiff Highball and tells her to go relax. Tiny turns on some smooth Jazz for her to listen to and he shuts the door so no one can bother her.

Sassy is one of Moms' cats, she meows to go into the bathroom so Tiny opens the door to let her in. Cochise and Nikita lie outside the bathroom door and won't let anyone disturb her.

"Detective Lorenzo, I think it's time for you to high tail it out of here," Ginger says to him.

"Okay, but I will have someone patrolling around the clock and watching over this house."

"Good night detective!!"

Mom gets out of the bath and Tiny has cooked her favorite dish shrimp and rice and has a bottle of wine waiting for her.

"Hey babe, I cooked you dinner."

"That's awful sweet of you Tiny, I'm starved, thank you."

"Mom, I hired Macc to get to the bottom of this

and find out what's going on."

"I don't know about this Shiloh; he works for your Uncle Vito. How can you be sure that we can trust him, your uncle is a sleazebag and in my book so is everyone he comes into contact with."

"Look mom, Macc has connections and I feel that he will find the answers we are looking for. The police aren't doing anything to help us so we need to go in another direction, just trust me on this will you?"

"Okay, I will but I don't like it one-bit Shiloh. I hope you know what you're getting yourself into."

"Well Tiny, dinner was very good, I think I'm going to turn in now." "Okay babe, I will be there in just a bit after I clean up the kitchen."

It took Tiny about an hour to clean up the kitchen and take him a shower as well and by the time he got to bed, Kitty was fast asleep and snoring.

CHAPTER 6

Macc starts with the man in the basement on his quest to find out who's trying to hurt Kitty.

"Okay you scumbag start talking or you're gonna start losing body parts real quick."

"Keep that crazy bitch away from me!"

"Why were you following Shiloh and who do you work for?"

"I'm dead if I tell you anything."

"You're dead if you don't tell me and it's going to be a slow and agonizing death. It's your choice."

"I'm dead either way so just kill me now."

"I'm going to ask you again, who do you work for?"

"Fuck you and spits in Macc's face."

Macc takes his knife and chops off one of his fingers.

"Now talk or your finger on your other hand gets chopped off."

"Fuck you and spits in his face again".

Macc grabs a pair of pliers and puts it around his nuts," now you're gonna tell me what I want to know or I'm gonna crack me some nuts."

"Okay, Okay I'll tell you, put the pliers away. His name is Rocco, he runs a head shop over on Grand and MLK. I don't know anything else he just paid me to follow the girl and take pictures and report back to him that's all I know I swear."

"If you're lying to me, I will find your family and they will die one by one slowly."

"I'm telling you the truth."

Macc takes out his knife and cuts his throat then puts his body in a sheet and carries him out and puts him in the trunk of his car... He chained two cinder blocks to his feet to weigh him down and dumped him into the Mississippi River.

Macc takes his car back to his crib and cleans it inside out to be sure there's nothing that can be traced back to him.

Macc has a white 1972 Cadillac Coupe Deville with '30s and Vogues with white rims. He heads on down to the head shop to see Roco only some other guy named Lenny was there.

"Hey, my man I'm looking for Rocco, he here?"

"Who wants to know?"

"Well since I'm the only one here and looks like I'm the only one asking my guess genius, would be me."

Lenny is 5'6" red curly hair down to his shoulders with a beard and mustache and has tattoos all over along with multiple piercings on his eyebrows, nose, lips, and ears. He has on a dirty old navy T-shirt with holes in it and a pair of jeans with holes in the knees.

"You the Fuzz?"

"Do I fucking look like the fuzz? Where's Rocco?"

"Not here!"

Macc pulls out his gun and points it at his head.

"I'm tired of fucking with you, now where's Rocco or I'm going to blow a hole in your head."

"I don't know man, don't shoot, he just said he would be back later on, not sure when and didn't say where he was going or when he would be back. I know he likes to go to the track over at Lincoln Speedway, maybe you can catch up with him there."

Macc puts his gun away," I'll be back if I don't find him." He jumps into his ride and heads over to the speedway. He gets to the speedway and parks then goes inside to look for Rocco. Macc and Rocco have known each other since they were kids.

Macc sees Vito and walks up to him.

"What's good Vito, my man?"

"What are you doing over here in these parts? I'm paying you to watch my niece and you can't do that from here."

"Relax man, it's all good, I got it covered."

"You better have because if anything happens to her I'm holding you responsible and you will pay the price."

Macc spots a black Camaro with tinted windows driving by slowly and looks like they are watching him and Vito.

"Well I have to bounce Vito, I'll holla at you later man."

"Okay, just remember what I said Macc."

Macc goes out to his ride and the black Camaro is gone. There was a note stuck on his windshield saying, "I've got my eye on you."

Macc knows Roco pretty well so he decides to check out the local tittie bars. He walks into Big Titties of America and there's Rocco right up in the front drunk as hell putting money in their G string.

Rocco is 5'10', short black hair, 195 pounds

with a beard and mustache with a tattoo on his forearm of Hankh. He drives a 1965 burgundy Buick Sklar with a graduation tassel hanging from his rear-view mirror.

Macc grabs a bottle of Hennessy and takes a seat at Rocco's table. "Hey Macc, it's good to see you. What brings you here?"

"Actually, I've been looking everywhere for you."

"Well, you found me so what can I do for you?"

"Word on the street is you put a tail on my girl Shiloh and her mom. Someone also tried to kidnap Kitty, I need some answers man. One of your flunkies sang like a canary."

"I don't know what you're talkin about Macc."

"Look, Rocco, don't fuck with me on this, you need to be straight with me we have known each other way too long. This is serious."

"Okay man, I'll tell you what I know. There are two guys, they are identical twins and they live over on the Southside on one of the state streets, I believe it's Michigan. Don't know the address but you can't miss it. It's a big purple house with a red door and fenced-in yard with two pit bulls. Well anyway, their names are Lefty on account he lost his arm when he had it hanging out the window when he and his brother were driving down the highway and a semi came flying by and cut it clean off and his twins' name is One Eye, on account he was making a pipe bomb one night and it blew up in his face causing him to go blind in one eye."

"What do they want with Kitty and Shiloh?"

"I'm not sure Macc, you're gonna have to ask them."

"Don't play with me Rocco. I know you hired some dirtbag to tail Shiloh and take pictures. Why?"

"Look man, I got myself into a bad situation and my bookie was putting the squeeze on me and said my debt would be cleared if I did a small job for him. I didn't ask any questions I did what he wanted. He was looking for something valuable I know but wouldn't tell me what it was and said the old lady had it in her possession that's all I know. I was in no situation to be questioning him."

"What's your bookie's name?"

"His name is Marcus, but they call him the Weasel. He's not hard to find he's a little queer, short, fat, and bald and looks like a weasel too."

Macc finishes his bottle of whiskey then takes off. He cruises down Michigan and sure enough, there's the purple house. He spots Lefty and one eye sitting on the porch then the door opens and out walks Vito. *"Now isn't that interesting,"* he says to himself wondering what his involvement is. It can't be good. So Macc waits down the street for Vito to leave then follows him.

Vito stops at Deaconess hospital and goes up to the fifth floor, room 5222. Macc watches the elevator to see what floor he gets off at then he takes the stairwell.

"Hey, I got here as soon as I could"? Vito says to a man with his face all bandaged up. "It won't be long now everything is coming all together, no one suspects a thing. That crazy old woman won't know what hit her. I got to go now but I'll be back soon to check on your progress."

Macc hides in one of the rooms as Vito leaves so he's not spotted and continues to follow Vito.

Vito goes down on Broadway to Foxy's Cat Houses. (A well-known whore house.) Everyone seems to know Vito well. Three girls escort him upstairs and two hours later Vito comes strolling out of the building. Macc then follows Vito back to his pad when he notices the black Camaro creeping down the street slowly, but it turns down an alley instead of going past the house.

Macc goes upstairs to talk to Shiloh and tells her everything he's found out tonight and what he saw.

"I can't believe my Uncle Vito is involved in all this mess."

"We don't know this for sure it could just be a coincidence. He loves you very much and wouldn't let anyone or anything hurt you."

"NO, but he would hurt mom.

"I can't and won't let him hurt my mom. He's gonna have to be stopped, I don't care what I have to do. This just doesn't make any sense. What in the hell is going on and what are they looking for? Macc please find out for me, I'm afraid for my mom. In the meantime, Ace and I will go get all the ammunition we need. I feel like we will be going to war real soon and I don't want to be caught with my pants down. I am going to protect my family with everything I got and if that means putting a bullet in my Uncle then that's what I will do. I'll catch up with you later Macc."

"I got you Shiloh, I will find out one way or another what's about to go down."

Mom and Ginger came up the stairs and went to mom's bedroom so they could listen to the tapes of Vito from the bug she planted.

"I got the ball rolling, shouldn't be much longer now. Everything's coming together, I stopped by the hospital today to see how much progress is being made. Everything is going as planned."

"That's Vito talking. I know his voice anywhere." Kitty says to Ginger. "Now what in the hell is he up to. We need to go to the hospital and see what he's up to, but what hospital he didn't say."

"Well, there's not that many hospitals in St. Louis so it shouldn't be that hard, but we don't even know what we are looking for Kitty, he doesn't give us a clue as to what progress he's talking about."

"That's okay I have a plan." "Ole boy this should be good."

Kitty looks out the window and sees Macc leaving. "Ginger, Macc is on the move, let's go, so they decide to follow him. He goes over to the racetrack to see if he can find the weasel. He asks a group of guys and they point to the cage where they make their bets. The weasel sees him coming and takes off running.

"Dammit, you little Leprechaun weasel son of a bitch I hate to run."

The weasel is running in and out of parked cars to get away. Macc has him cornered in between a couple of cars. "I just need to talk to you." The weasel runs between Macc's legs and opens one of the parked car doors and climbs through and goes to the other door and climbs out, he goes through about four or five cars and finally gets to his little red bug and screeches away. Macc runs back to his car and goes after him.

"What in the Hell," Macc says. Here comes Kitty and Ginger on their bikes chasing the weasel.

"Get the hell out of here Kitty you're going to get hurt, Shiloh will be pissed if you lady's got hurt now back off I got this."

"We aren't going anywhere we saw how you handled it back there, pretty smooth Macc. So smooth in fact that the little weasel slipped right through your legs." (Kitty and Ginger start laughing.)

While Kitty and Macc are arguing Ginger is hot on his trail. The weasel pulls out his gun and shoots at Ginger, but she dodges it and he misses and shoots the tire out of another car causing him to lose control and flip over causing other cars to crash into each other. The car that flipped is leaking gasoline, Macc stops and runs over to the car and pulls a guy from the vehicle before it blows, as they are running from the car there is a big explosion and throws them in the air and they come down hard onto the pavement.

Kitty and Ginger are still on the weasel's tail. Ginger on one side and Kitty on the other side of his car flying down seventh street. Here comes Macc from behind and rams him in the ass. Ginger and Kitty take out their guns and Ginger shoots the driver's front tire and Kitty shoots out the passenger rear tire. He loses control and runs into a fire hydrant and busts it wide open and water is shooting straight up in the air. His airbag opens so he takes his knife and cuts it so he can get out now the seatbelt won't release so he cuts the belt and now the door is jammed and won't open so he climbs out the window and starts to run.

"Dammit, this little dude just doesn't stop," Macc says.

Ginger and Kitty run after him and tackle him to the ground. Kitty zapps him with her stun gun, he ain't going nowhere now.

"Damn we make a great team Kitty. Since we took him down he's our prisoner."

"Macc won't like that one-bit Ginger."

"To hell with Macc, the weasel slipped right through his legs Kit."

"I agree with you, but I don't think Macc will just hand him over to us."

"He doesn't have to, just leave it to me."

Macc jumps out of his car and goes over to the weasel, "I hate to run you little dumb shit and pulls him up and throws him in the car".

"Okay Macc, we need to talk," Kitty says. "Since Ginger and I are the ones who actually took him down, we are going to take it from here."

"NO! That's not how it works Kitty. I'm going to jump into my ride and take him to my place, we are not playing a game of cops and robbers here this is serious shit and you ladies can get seriously hurt."

Macc hears tires screeching and he turns around only to see the tail end of his car going down the road. "What the hell! Ginger just stole my damn car and kidnapped the weasel."

Kitty starts smiling and yelling at Ginger "you go girl and don't look back."

"So that was your plan to distract me so Ginger can hijack my car and the weasel."

"No, I had no idea she was going to do that but I'm glad she did. It was very clear and evident that you weren't going to hand him over to us."

"What were you going to do, strap him to your bikes? How were you planning on taking him, have you thought about that? You women are making my job harder to do, always interfering. Now, where is she taking him?"

"I don't know where she is taking him but you're an incompetent fool and I don't know why Shiloh hired you in the first place. She needs her head examined, we were the ones who took him down and not you, so therefore, the balls in our court so deal with it."

"I'll deal with it alright; you lady's better stay out of my way or you will regret it.

I'm not playing with you two anymore."

"Did you just threaten us?"

"No, it's a promise, now back the fuck off and I

mean it!!"

"Bring it, I got something for you."

CHAPTER 7

Ginger paged Kitty so she could call her back and find out where she took the weasel so they could meet up and take care of business.

Kitty received the page and stopped right away at a local 7-eleven store on Jefferson and called the number on her pager.

"Thank God you called Kitty, I'm at Katz meet me here right away."

"I'm on my way Ginger, hang tight."

Kitty got back on her bike and took off to Hwy 44 and headed east. It started raining and thundering and Kitty was doing about 70 mph when she came to a traffic jam. There was an accident and they had the Hwy blocked off. All kinds of emergency vehicles were on the scene (ambulances, fire trucks, and police cars.) The posted speed limit is 55 mph and Kitty was doing well over. Kitty started riding on the shoulder trying to get through. Ginger is paging her again wondering what is taking so long. This time she puts 911 behind the number so she knows it's an emergency. Kitty has no way to get around the accident and traffic is backed up so she crosses over on the other side of the Hwy and starts going the wrong way in traffic to hurry and get to Ginger, she is weaving in and out of traffic, and cars are honking and yelling at her and cussing. Kitty manages to get off the highway and arrives at Katz shortly after.

Kitty pulls around back and sees Ginger waiting in the car.

Ginger jumps out of the car, “Thank God, I was starting to get worried.”

“Oh my God there was an accident at 44 and 55, a tractor-trailer was overturned, and the highway was blocked off. Traffic is crazy, it was hell getting here but I wasn’t going to let anything get in my way.”

“Okay, Kitty let’s take this little weasel to the basement. I put a pillowcase over his head so he couldn’t see where I was taking him, and I cuffed his hands behind his back.”

“Alright, let’s do this! Let’s take care of this scumbag once and for all.”

Kitty opens the trunk and they each grab an arm and pull him out. The storm is crazy, it’s raining so hard and the lightning struck an electric pole and knocked out the power on the whole street.

“Oh my God Kitty, it’s pitch black out here, I

can't see two feet in front of me." Kitty shoves a gun in the weasel's side. "Let's go and don't try anything funny."

Ginger trips over a fallen branch and the weasel trips over Ginger then Kitty falls and all three of them are wrestling to get up.

"Dammit the hell, Zap his ass Kitty."

Kitty takes out her stun gun and zaps him in the ass.

"Woza not me, wrong ass."

The weasel is laughing so hard he's crying.

"Oh my God I'm so sorry Ginger. It's so damn dark out here I can't see a thing."

"Ooh wee what's that smell?"

"It was me Kitty, when you zapped my ass I farted and almost peed on myself."

"Yea, right in my face too. Smells like you shit in your pants, Damn." The weasel says to Ginger.

"No, but I'll shit on you if you don't cooperate here."

Kitty and Ginger both manage to get up and grab the weasel to his feet. They walk slowly up to the door of Katz and Ginger opens the door and turns on the lights. When the electricity goes out the generator automatically kicks on.

“Let’s take him down to the cellar Ginger, no one ever goes down there.”

CHAPTER 8

Ace and Shiloh head on over to the east side to meet some gun runners so they will be ready for anything that's about to go down. They arrive underneath the Stargate Bridge at midnight. Shiloh and Ace get out of their car and walk about 10 yards to meet the runners.

"Giovanni, how ya been man?" Shiloh, says.

"Shiloh, it's been a long time. These are my boys, Salvatore known as the Iceman, Bugsy known as Fingers, Luigi known as the Owl, and Anthony known as Shoes."

"This is Ace, my partner. We served in the Military together."

Giovani opened his trunk, he has an arsenal, all types of guns, hand grenades, dynamite, and some homemade bombs.

"Damn "G" how much are we talking about here?"

"$10,000, that's the best I can do for you Shiloh." "Okay, you got yourself a deal."

Ace goes to the car and grabs a duffel bag with the money and hands it to Giovani, he opens the bag and counts the money then hands over the merchandise.

“Thanks “G”, Later.

“Take care of yourself Shiloh and be careful. If you ever need anything you know how to get in touch with me. Hit me up.”

“I sure will and thanks for everything.”

Ace and Shiloh head back to the crib and Macc is sitting on the porch waiting for them and he isn’t looking very happy.

Shiloh gets out of the car and says, “hey Macc, tell me you found out something.” “We need to talk upstairs. You’re damn mother and that Ginger are out of control and they keep interfering with me trying to do my job. Ginger stole my truck with the weasel in it and then your mom takes off shortly after.”

WHAT? ARE YOU SERIOUS!!! I’m sorry Macc I will find them and get your car back. I will also straighten this all out.

I sure hope you do Shiloh. Everywhere I go there they are. I have a few other leads that I’m gonna follow up on. I'll catch up with you later.

“Okay Macc and thank you.”

Shiloh hears a knock at the door, so Ace goes downstairs to answer it. "Who is it?" Shiloh yells.

"It's Detective Lorenzo."

"Okay send him up."

Ace yells back to her, "I'll be back in a little while, I have something to take care of."

"What can I do for you, detective?"

"Just in the neighborhood so I thought I would stop in and check on you to see how you are doing"

"Thank you that was very thoughtful of you."

"I was on my way to grab a bite to eat, would you like to accompany me."

"I would love to detective, I'm famished."

"Great, I know this little Mexican place down on Cherokee Street we can go to."

"Sounds good, I could use a Margarita, I've had a very rough day. I just need a quick minute to take a shower and change. Make yourself comfortable."

Shiloh gets dressed and 30 minutes later comes walking out wearing a form-fitting short red dress with black sandals that lace up and her long black hair flowing down freely. She gives Cochise his ointment and medicine and takes him out to the bathroom and gets him comfortable for the rest of the night and then she feeds mom's five cats.

"Okay detective I'm ready."

Lorenzo stands up and says "Wow you look amazing"

"Thank you, detective, that's very nice of you to say."

"Please call me Eddie."

"Alright Eddie shall we go then?"

Eddie and Shiloh head downstairs to Eddie's car, a beautiful 1963 blue Corvair convertible.

"Nice car detective! I mean Eddie."

"Thanks."

Eddie opens the passenger car door and Shiloh gets in.

"What a gentleman you are, thank you."

"My pleasure Shiloh."

Eddie gets in and drives to Cherokee Street and they arrive at Tres Margaritas.

Eddie has the valet porter park the car but not before he walks around the car to open Shiloh's door for her and takes her by the hand to help her out.

Eddie and Shiloh walk into the restaurant and get greeted immediately.

"Hola, ¿Cuántos hoy?" (How many today?)

"Dos." (Two).

"¿Por aqui?" (Right this way.)

"¿Que puedo traerte de beber?" (What can I get you to drink?)

"Dos Margaritas." (Two Margaritas.)

The waiter was back in five minutes with our chips and two Margaritas.

"¿Estás listo con tu orden?" (Are you ready with your order?)

"Si." (yes.)

"Tomaré la fajita de carne y la señora tomará la fajita de pollo." (I will take the steak fajita and the lady will take the chicken fajita.)

"Gracias." (Thank you,)

"Muy bien senor, lo sacaré lo más rápido." (Very good sir I'll have it out as quickly as possible.)

"This is a very nice place and their Margaritas are to die for."

Eddie went up to one of the musicians and gave him a hundred-dollar bill to come to his table and sing to Shiloh and serenade her.

"This is so lovely. Did you arrange this?"

"I'm glad you like it. You deserve to be spoiled

and pampered."

"Lord knows it's been a long while since anyone has done that for me."

"I find that hard to believe, you are such a beautiful woman."

The waiter arrives with their dinner and lets them know the plates are very hot. "Gracias." (Thank you.)

"De nada." (You're welcome.)

"Dinner was fantastic Eddie, actually the whole evening is. Thank you, I needed this for an end to my night."

"The night doesn't have to end yet Shiloh. How do you feel about going dancing? There's this place not far from here I think you'll like, It's called the Casablanca Ballroom."

"Ooh that sounds great, I'd love to."

Eddie and Shiloh go to the ballroom and Shiloh's eyes light up." This place is amazing."

The ballroom has high cathedral ceilings with a round staircase going to the second floor. There are two bars downstairs and one upstairs with two huge dance floors and live music nightly. The blues are playing on one floor and classical playing on the other floor. The lighting is very dim, and the tables have lavender satin tablecloths with candles on each one. The waitress comes to your table to take your drink orders or any appetizers you may want very, very elegant.

They sat at a nice cozy table off to the side in the back. They talked, laughed, drank, and danced the night away.

The last dance of the night was a slow song. Eddie grabs her at the waist and draws her body so close to him that he could hear her heart beating faster and faster. He kisses her on the ear then on the neck and then a slow and passionate kiss and she responds right back with a long but slow passionate kiss. They stop for a moment and look at each other in the eyes and smile.

"Are you ready to get out of here?"

"Yes."

The valet porter drives his car around and opens the door for Shiloh and Eddie gives a nice tip.

"The night is still young Shiloh, it's only 1:30 in the morning and I don't want our night to end. Let's go back to my place for a nightcap, shall we?"

Yes, that would be nice. I'm having a really

good time with you. It's been an amazing night.

As they drive to Eddie's house, they are both sitting quietly in their own thoughts

"She is just so beautiful sitting there in her red dress and nice tan long legs and her long hair blowing in the wind. The kiss we shared was so delicious, I wonder how she would respond if I pulled the car over and stole another kiss."

"Damn he's fine as hell, is this just a one-night affair for him or is he wanting more? What does he expect is going to happen?Okay, you are overthinking again whatever happens just go with it. Oh my God, that kiss was so wonderful, I can't even remember the last time someone kissed me like that."

Eddie pulls the car over and pulls Shiloh close to him and starts kissing her and it's getting pretty heated fast. He unzips the back of her dress and she starts to unbutton his shirt but she can't quite get it so she rips it off and starts to unbuckle his belt.

"What a Tiger you are!!"

Eddie looks in his rear-view mirror and sees the police roll up and shines a spotlight on them.

The officer walks up slowly to the car. "Is everything okay here?"

"Yes, just fine officer Dickwad."

The officer takes a closer look.

"Detective Lorenzo? I almost didn't recognize you without your clothes on."

"Very funny Dickwad. It's hot so I just took my shirt off."

"I guess I would be hot too if I had a hot little number sitting next to me half-dressed. Well, I'll let you get back to business and he whispers in the detective's ear, I'd take it to the bedroom and tap that ass."

"Thanks Officer Dickwad, I'll see you in the morning."

"It's all good detective the boys down at the precinct will understand if you're late."

Eddie pulls back onto the highway and Shiloh is still hot and bothered so she climbs on his lap and straddles him and starts kissing his ear and neck then starts sucking his neck. She can feel his excitement and arousal. Shiloh takes her breast out of her dress and puts them in his face. He's trying very hard to concentrate on the road and not to have an accident.

A car full of young kids in their twenties pulls up alongside and starts cheering. One girl yells "Get it

Big Daddy," and a boy yells "ride it, Mamma," Yeah! Another boy yells "would you look at the boobs on that babe, he's one lucky guy."

Eddie gets off the highway and makes a few turns and pulls into his driveway.They get out of the car and Eddie picks her up and carries her up to the house and into his bedroom. He whispers in her ear "Those kids were right about one thing, I am a very lucky man. I don't think I've ever felt this way with any other woman before."

He slips off her dress and lets it fall to the floor. She then begins to take his belt off and unzips his pants and pulls them off. He throws her on the bed kissing her whole body and his hands caressing every inch of her. I want to pleasure you and make you feel good. "Just tell me what you want me to do and I'll do it."

She lets out a soft but sexy moan," you are doing just fine, you don't need me to tell you anything, just don't stop." Shiloh rolls over on top of him and starts rolling her tongue up his inner thigh giving him goosebumps then starts caressing his privates. She gets him aroused and they make love for an hour before falling asleep.

Shiloh wakes up to the smell of coffee brewing and bacon cooking. She gets dressed and goes into the kitchen.

"Wow, you are up early, smells good, what are you cooking?"

"I'm cooking eggs, bacon, sausage patties, and hash browns with peppers and onions. I hope you're hungry ".

"Yes, I'm starved."

"What would you like to drink, I have coffee, tea, milk, hot chocolate, kool-aid, or orange juice?"

"I'll have some orange juice, thanks."

"Coming right up dear. Eddie pours a glass of orange juice and kisses her on the forehead."

He fixes them both a plate and they both sit down to eat. Eddie says a prayer before they begin.

"Is there anything you can't do? This breakfast is amazing."

"Well, I do take pride in everything I do."

They finish eating and Shiloh gets up to do the dishes.

"You are my guest. I will take care of the dishes."

"No Eddie, you have done so much for me

already, the least I can do is clean up the kitchen, I insist."

"Okay if you insist, I never argue with a woman."

"Wow is he for real? I could get used to this very quickly, he's a smooth operator that's for sure."

While Shiloh is doing the dishes, Eddie comes up behind her and wraps his arms around her waist. "When can I see you again?"

"I'm not sure Eddie, I have so much on my plate right now. I don't know if I'm coming or going sometimes. I do want to see you again, but my life is just so complicated right now. We just have to play it by ear and see what happens."

"Okay, fair enough but if there's anything I can do, don't hesitate to ask."

"I just want to find out who's behind everything that's been happening to my family."

"I promise you we will find out and I will take care of it."

"Okay, thank you."

"I really need to be getting home now, would you mind taking me?"

"Not at all." They get in the car and Eddie takes her home and double parks in front of her house.

"Thanks Eddie for an incredible evening," she leans in and gives him a long passionate kiss and then gets out of the car and goes upstairs.

Ace is waiting in the living room looking pretty upset. "Where have you been?

I've been worried sick about you! I was getting ready to call the good detective here but I see it appears you were with him all night."

"We went to dinner then dancing and had a few drinks, nothing major."

"You look different."

"What do you mean?"

"You have a glow about you, did you sleep with him?"

"I really don't think that's any of your business."

"Dammit, Shiloh don't do this."

"What am I doing?"

"I saw the kiss when he dropped you off, it didn't look like nothing to me, it looked very intimate."

"What! Are you spying on me now?"

"NO! I just happened to be looking out when Romeo pulled up."

"Do I sense a little jealousy going on here? That's so sweet."

Ace grabs Shiloh and pulls her hard against him.

"Ace, what are you doing? We are not an item, that was a thing in our past."

"I'm not going to let him take the only woman I've ever loved away from me and he kisses her hard then softens up and she kisses him back."

"I need some time and space to think Ace. Please don't make this awkward, I'm going to take a long hot bath and relax now before I have to go find mom and see what she is up to."

CHAPTER 9

Vito heads out the door to go take care of some business when he sees Macc pull up.

"Where the hell have you been? I'm paying you to watch my niece."

"I am "V" she spent the night at that cops house."

"Get in the car you're coming with us."

Macc gets in the Limo with Vito and doesn't say a word. They head up Wyoming and hung a left-down grand and pull up at the hospital.

"Wait in the car Macc, I'll only be a few minutes."

"What's good Vito? Someone sick or hurt?"

Vito ignores him and goes into the hospital and gets in the elevator and hits the button for the fifth floor.

"Hey man, I'll be back. I gotta go take a leak. " Macc jumps out of the car and takes the stairs up to the fifth floor.

Vito reaches the door and says, "It's time."

The doctor comes in to remove the bandages and starts cutting them off slowly.

"Looking pretty good."

He turns around and Vito takes one look at him and says, "Now that's what I call a work of art."

The doctor gives him a mirror and he stares for a long minute.

There's a loud crash in the hallway so Vito throws Jack a gun and they both go to investigate.

A nurse said she saw a black stocky man running down the hallway. "I think he was eavesdropping but whatever he saw or heard must have spooked him."

"What makes you say that?".

"Just by the way he backed up and ran into my cart like he couldn't get out of here fast enough."

"I bet Macc followed me up here."

"We can't let him ruin this for us, we need to take him out now."

"No, not yet, we need to find out what he knows first."

Macc gets back to the car and the driver says, "What's wrong with you?"

"Looks like you've seen a ghost or something."

"No, just not feeling too good right now, I think I might be coming down with something I'm not sure."

"Maybe you need to go get checked out."

"Yeah, maybe."

Vito and Jack come out of the hospital and jump into the back of the Limo one on each side of Macc.

"You are looking kind of pale Macc, you okay?"

Antonio the driver says, "Your man back there isn't feeling too hot. He thinks he might be coming down with something."

"Really! Sorry to hear that."

"Maybe you should just drop me off at the crib and I'll catch up with you later."

"No!" "We have a lot of work to do Macc."

"Jack here will be working with us."

The Limo pulls up in the back of Vito's pad and they all go in the back way so no one can see them go inside the house.

Everyone goes into the house and sits down at the kitchen table and Vito pours a round of drinks when the doorbell rings. Vito answers the door and it's some little girls selling girl scout cookies. He gives them a 100-dollar bill and buys them out and tells them to beat it.

Jack is staring at Macc and making him really

uncomfortable. Macc doesn't say anything because he's not sure what he is dealing with and he knows he is in a dangerous situation.

Vito sits back down at the table and starts to play poker and says to Macc, "You don't look too good, you okay?"

"No, not really, I think I need to go home and get some rest. I'll check back in with you later man."

"Okay, be back here in the morning."

"I will," as Macc is leaving Lefty and one eye show up and they all stare at each other.

Lefty says, "hey man don't I know you?"

"Naw, I don't think so."

Lefty says, "Is that your ride?"

"Yeah, I gotta bounce."

Lefty and One Eye walk into Vito's house. Vito stands up to shake their hands and introduces them to Jack.

Lefty asks, "Who was the guy that just left your house?" "Does he work for you?"

"Yeah, why do you ask?"

"I'm pretty sure he drove by our house real slow the day that you were there." "Are you sure about this?"

"Yes."

Jack says, "I knew I should have taken him out back at the hospital."

"We will get to the bottom of this when he gets here tomorrow. In the meantime, let's party." One Eye turns up the music, Jack pulls out the drugs and Lefty starts pouring shots and making drinks.

Vito has a girl on each arm and starts heading for the hot tub outback. All three get in the tub and Vito has drinks and music and a couple of lines of coke. The two girls start kissing each other then they start kissing Vito, all of a sudden, the door opens, and everyone stares. A tall beautiful woman walks in with a dark tan and long brown hair with a tattoo of a black widow on her back wearing nothing but her birthday suit, she steps into the hot tub and moves towards the girls and brushes up against their bodies and Vito says, "Lucinda what are you doing here?" She gives him a long hard kiss getting him very excited.

"I came to party Vito, it's way overdue."

Vito is not too sure that is why Lucinda really came tonight. Something big is about to go down he can feel it.

Lucinda does a few lines and is feeling no pain

and starts to make out with both girls. She whispers in their ear and they both grab a towel and leave quickly. Lucinda moves closer to Vito and rubs her hands over the front of his shorts feeling his arousal. She starts to kiss his neck then she puts her hands down his shorts and squeezes his balls and bites his ear and says, "Tell me you found the merchandise."

"No, not yet Lucinda, but we will, it's only a matter of time. We are closing in." "Time is something we don't have, now let's get it done."

The door opens slowly and in walks Jack. Lucinda stands up and walks over to him. "Well now, who do we have here?"

Vito says, "This is Jack."

He walks over and takes her hand and kisses it," such a beautiful creature."

She brushes her lips against his and signals for Vito to leave. She grabs Jack by the hand and leads him into the hot tub. They both do a line and take a couple of shots of Jack Daniels.

Jack grabs her breasts and starts kissing them, he then starts caressing her body and turns her around and runs his tongue along her spine then they start to have sex.

She looks at him and says, “I must go now but we will see each other again very soon.”

Lucinda gets dressed and walks into the Foyer where Vito is and she says, “I want results Vito, and soon.”

“Yes, I’m on it as we speak.”

“You better be, and she leaves.”

In walks Jack with a smile on his face.

Vito says, “We need to talk. “They go down to the basement and Duke follows them.

“We need to find Kitty and find out what she knows and where my brother hid the stuff. If we don’t find it real soon the Black Widow will have our heads.”

“The Black Widow?”

“Yes, Lucinda is known as the Black Widow. She is a very powerful woman and you don’t want to cross her. I don’t want to know what went on out in the hot tub but once she gets her hooks into you that’s it you belong to her and the only way out is a body bag.”

“Okay, Jack, you go over to the Eastside to find kitty and I will go see Macc.”

They both head out and Duke jumps in Vito’s car and goes with him.

CHAPTER 10

Macc wakes up and looks across the room and sees Vito sitting in a chair with a gun and Duke at his side.

“What are you doing here? I thought I was supposed to meet you at your pad this morning.”

“There’s been a change of plans. I had a few visitors when you left last night. It seems you have been very busy following me around everywhere so you’d better start explaining fast before I let Duke loose on you.” Duke starts to growl and bare his teeth.

“It’s not what you think. Shiloh hired me to find out who’s behind all the shit that's been happening to her mom and that’s it, I swear man.”

“Where’s Kitty now? I don’t know I haven’t seen her.

” Duke bites Macc in the nuts and won’t let go.

“You better talk Macc before Duke crushes your nuts.”

“Okay, Okay call him off.”

Duke heal! He lets go and sits.

“I saw Kitty two days ago, I went to talk to the weasel, and he ran so I chased him, and out of nowhere here comes Ginger and Kitty on their bikes. They screwed everything up. I caught up with the weasel and put him in my car and when Kitty and I were arguing Ginger stole my ride with the weasel in it and that's the last time I saw them."

Vito starts laughing." You mean to tell me that you got outsmarted by two old ladies. Where did they take him?"

"I don't know, they didn't exactly tell me their plans."

"Get dressed, we are going to find them. We will start at their club first."

Jack is already at the club and it's all dark and it appears no one is there. He pulls out his gun and starts looking around but doesn't see anyone.

Vito and Macc pull up and get out with their guns drawn and start looking around.

Shilo shows up at the club and sees Vito's car so she hides her car and grabs her gun then climbs on the roof and crawls on her stomach so she's not seen.

Macc says," No one is here I think we should go." He looks up and sees Shiloh, but he doesn't say anything.

Jack sets fire to the dumpster in the back then they all get in their cars and leave.

Shiloh jumps off the roof and runs inside to get the fire extinguisher before the fire spreads to the building. She managed to keep it under control and puts it out. She goes over to the cellar because she figures that is where her mom and Ginger are hiding out with the weasel. She lifts the cellar door and walks down the long dark stairs and the walls have cracks and holes crawling with bugs and spider webs everywhere she gets to the bottom of the stairs and there is a lot of standing water with rats running around and as she gets a little farther she sees another door so she opens it slowly and she sees Ginger, Kitty, and the weasel. “Mom what are you doing here? Vito and a couple of his thugs were topside with guns looking for you and one of them set fire to the dumpster but I managed to control it and put it out, good thing I was up on the roof where I could see what was happening otherwise it could have spread to the club.”

“That damn Vito, I’m going to get him if it’s the last thing I do.”

“Okay mom, we need a plan.”

"So, you're finally going to team up with me so we can get these bastards."

"Yes, but first we got to find out what they are after so bad, if we can find that out everything else should fall into place hopefully."

"Now we need to deal with this little weasel." They all turn to look at the weasel who is chained up on a spinning wheel with his arms and legs stretched out as far as they can go and just wearing his underwear.

Shiloh walks over to him and demands to know what is going on and why everyone is after her mom. He refuses to talk so Shiloh punches him in the face with her brass knuckles then take a bottle of water and just pours it down his throat practically drowning him then she takes out her gun and puts it in his mouth and says, "If you don't tell me what I need to know in the next 30 seconds I'm going to pull this trigger."

"Okay!"

"What are they looking for?"

"There's evidence out there somewhere that could put them away for life along with members of the cartel and they won't stop until they get what they want."

"What's that got to do with my mom??"

"Kitty's late husband had the evidence and they believe he passed it along to her."

"I think we would know if she had evidence like that."

"Not necessarily, he could have hidden it somewhere and not told her or anyone and she might have it but not know she has it."

Ginger gets dizzy and starts to fall but kitty catches her. "Are you okay Ginger, do you need some water."

"No, I'm fine I just had a flashback of me being at the club and I was listening to a conversation but I can't remember what it was about but then someone came up behind me with a gun and I ducked and gave him a roundhouse kick then I remember fighting with him trying to get the gun and it went off and that's all I remember."

"Okay, that's good Ginger at least you're starting to remember. The doctor said it would eventually come to you, but it may be in bits and pieces."

"I know but I feel like I know something that

could help but I can't remember. I'm sorry Kitty."

"It's okay honey, you will remember in time."

The weasel gives Ginger a funny look and says, "You really don't remember anything do you?"

Kitty walks over to the weasel with a pair of pliers and puts it around his tongue and says, "If you don't tell me what you know about what happened to Ginger, I am going to cut your tongue out."

"Alright, damn, all i know is that she walked up on a conversation that wasn't meant for her ears and she got caught."

"Who was having the conversation and what was it about?"

"Shiloh's man Ace and Mad Dog. Ace came back here to help find the evidence they need to save their asses except there was one problem: Mad Dogs daughter walked up on you and she was the one that stopped you except you were supposed to be dead."

"I don't believe you. Ace isn't involved."

"Do you really think it was a coincidence that he showed up when he did with this story that he was here to help you and showing his concern. He was made an offer that was too good to pass up so if it meant betraying the woman he loved well then so be it."

"Who is Mad Dog's daughter?"

"Well, that's the kicker, she works for Kitty."

"Who the hell is she?"

"It's one of your best pole dancers, Fiona."

"You're lying, I don't believe you, she was being harassed by a man at the time." "This was actually before then; it just took her that long to make her way out to you."

Shiloh says, "Okay girls let's go we have business to take care of."

"Wait! What about me, you can't just leave me here I told you what you wanted to know."

They all three walk away without looking back. Kitty says, "So what's the plan Shiloh?"

"I'm not sure yet, I'm just going to go on like I don't know anything, so we don't tip them off. We need to look for the evidence ourselves and find it before they do. We just need to watch our backs and each other's backs as well. Anyone gets in your way shoot them and ask questions later. Now let's go home and figure out our next course of action."

They all arrive back at the house, but Shiloh decides to knock on Vito's door. Vito answers the door," Shiloh what a surprise is everything ok?"

"I'm not sure Uncle Vito can I come in for a bit."

"Sure, come on in. Can I make you a drink?"

"That would be great. I sure could use one, can you make it a double."

"Have you found out anything yet Uncle Vito about who's behind everything that has been happening? It's really taking a toll on me mentally."

"Not yet sweetheart but I will, you can count on that."

"Ginger's memory is starting to come back slowly maybe we might find out something when it does."

"That's great Shiloh. Where's Ginger at now."

"I'm not sure, why?"

"I was thinking maybe she should stay close to you in case her memory comes back. She shouldn't be alone because you don't know what she went through."

"You're right Vito but I'm not sure where she is at right now probably with mom somewhere. Well thanks for the drink Uncle Vito I'm going to go upstairs now and go to bed."

"Okay, goodnight. I will let you know when I

find out anything."

"Thanks."

Shiloh goes upstairs and Ace is waiting for her. "Hi babe, can we talk? I hate the way we left things earlier and I want to make it right. I just love you so much and when I saw you kiss the detective, I guess I just got a little jealous."

Kitty comes running out of her room, "you did what Shiloh? Did I hear him say you kissed that big hunk of a detective?"

"Yes mother, we went out to eat and I had a rough day, so we went dancing. It was a great end to an awful day."

"Ace, can we talk later I'm pretty tired and need some sleep." Sure thing babe, and he kisses her on the forehead.

Kitty and Ginger go straight to Kitty's room so they can start listening in on Vito.

Shiloh steps out of her room quietly through the balcony so Ace wouldn't be able to hear her, now the three of them are listening in on Vito.

Vito is talking and saying they need to get a grip on things before the Black Widow comes back. Fiona, you work on Ginger and see how much she remembers, if she gets out of hand kill her. Jack, you take care of Kitty and Ace you work on Shiloh. Macc you keep searching and I don't care what you have to do but find it. We don't have much time now let's go.

Shiloh takes charge, "Okay girls we are about to throw down. It's going to get ugly. I can't believe Ace is in this with Vito and who's this Jack and what's his involvement. The Weasel said Fiona is Mad Dog's Daughter."

Ginger says, "I heard Fiona call Jack (Dad), you don't suppose Jack is Mad Dog, do you?"

Kitty says, "I don't know, but that does make sense now why Vito kept going to the hospital and visiting someone. I bet it was Mad Dog, he had plastic surgery so no one could recognize him and then changed his name.'

"Okay, so here's the plan," Shiloh says.

CHAPTER 11

Kitty hears a noise at 4:00 a.m., it's the front door opening and footsteps slowly coming up the stairs, she grabs her gun and wakes up Shiloh and she grabs her shotgun, as he reaches the top stair Kitty yells, "Freeze dirtbag" and Shiloh's gun is pointed at his head.

He drops his bag and throws his hands up and says, "Damn Mom, what the hell is going on here?"

"Daryl? Oh my God! Come here and give me some sugar. I can't believe my baby boy is home from the war. Just look at you, why didn't you tell me you were coming home? I would have picked you up from the airport."

"I wanted to surprise you."

Shiloh says, "Well you sure in the hell did that alright." (she laughs). "Come here little brother and hug me. I've missed you so much. I'm so glad you're home."

"So am I, now do either of you want to tell me what in the hell is going on around here?"

Daryl is bald, 5'10", and 180 pounds with baby blue eyes. He was drafted into the Military in June of

1960. Vietnam started in November of 1955. When the men turned 18, they had to register with the selective service. During his time in the Military, he became an Officer and a Fighter Pilot, he was also one of the top snipers in his unit. He received the Purple Heart from the President of the United States when he was wounded in the war. He lost two of his fingers and his left leg was amputated, he now wears a prosthesis.

"Okay, let's go into the living room and I will make some coffee and we can talk, and we will fill you in on everything that's been happening around here."

Shiloh and Kitty filled Daryl in on everything that has been going on.

Ace walks in and goes over to Shiloh and kisses her on the forehead then looks over at Daryl and says, "Who do we have here?"

Daryl stands up and holds out his hand and they shake hands. "I'm Daryl, Shiloh's brother."

"Hi Daryl, I'm Ace, a good friend of Shiloh's nice to meet you. How long are you here for?"

Shiloh and Kitty give each other that look, like some friend, with friends like that who needs enemies.

"I'm home for good now. What about you? How long are you here for?"

"I just came to visit an old friend; I've missed her so much and thought she could use some help."

"What does my sister need help with? I'm here now so I can help her with whatever she needs so thank you for being here for her, but I can take it from here."

"Well, I'm not going anywhere, I'm going to see things through till the end. I happen to love this woman with all my heart and I'm going to protect her with everything I've got."

There's a knock at the door and Cochise and Nikita start barking and run to the door and continue barking.

Shiloh goes to answer the door and it's detective Lorenzo." Hi Eddie, what a surprise and he gives her a big hug and kiss. Come on in, what brings you over this way?"

"I was just in the neighborhood and wanted to see you." They walk upstairs and Eddie says, "Looks like you have a full house this morning."

Eddie walks over to Daryl and shakes his hand and says, "Hi I'm detective Lorenzo."

Daryl stands up and says, “I’m Daryl, Shiloh’s brother.”

“I’ve heard a lot about you, welcome home, and thank you for your service.” “Thank you, and it’s great to be home.”

Ace says, “Well if it isn’t Mr. Loverboy.”

“Good Morning to you too Ace.” (smiling)

“Would you like a cup of coffee detective,” says Kitty. “Yes ma’am, that would be great, and thank you.”

Kitty brings the detective’s coffee and hands it to him and says,” It’s always a pleasure to see you.”

Ginger comes walking in and says, “Daryl, oh my God and rushes over to give him a hug. Welcome home and she kisses him on the cheek.” Hello detective, it’s great to see such a handsome face in the morning. What brings you here so bright and early this morning? Not that I mind, it’s a great way to start my day making me all tingling inside.” (She laughs)

Ginger has always been a big flirt; she loves the male species.

Ace stands up and says, “Wow, you women making such a fuss over this guy makes me sick, I will see you later Shiloh I have some things I need to take care of." Kitty says, "Shiloh, me and Ginger have to run also, we are going over to see Dillan."

"Okay Mom, please be careful."

"Careful is my middle name sweetheart."

Daryl and Eddie both stand up as the two women leave.

Daryl says, "Shiloh, I need to go and get some sleep, I've had a long flight and I'm pretty exhausted. It was nice meeting you, detective."

"Likewise, and call me Eddie."

"Okay baby brother, I will talk to you when you wake up."

Eddie says, "Looks like it's just me and you kid, alone at last. He starts kissing her neck. I've missed you and can't stop thinking about you."

"Eddie I can't right now, I'm sorry. I just found out some really disturbing news and I really can't believe it."

"What is it, babe? Let me know so I can help." Shiloh begins to tell him what she heard.

"You need to have him go to a hotel when he gets back."

"I can't because he will become suspicious."

"No, not really, now that your brother is home

just tell him you need the space for him now."

"They are out for blood Eddie; I can't risk it. I need to be close to him until I figure this all out. I appreciate your concern, but I can handle him. Trust me."

"Okay babe, but I will not be far, you can count on that. Together we will get to the bottom of this."

"Thank you and she kisses him. I will call you later Eddie."

"Alright but be careful. I know you won't listen to me and back off and let me handle it so be careful."

"I will don't you worry, I have some tricks up my sleeve. (She laughs). Bye Eddie I will keep in touch, I promise."

Eddie leaves so Shiloh takes a shower and gets dressed and takes Nikita and Cochise out for a walk while she thinks things through.

CHAPTER 12

Daryl wakes up and looks around the house and everyone is gone. He takes a shower, gets dressed, and puts on a nice Armani blue suit with a red tie, his black wingtip shoes, and his gold Rolex watch with diamonds all around it. He takes a cab to a car dealership on Grand and Chippewa and buys himself a red 1974 Cadillac Eldorado Convertible.

He drives over to Katz on the East Side to see Kitty but when he gets there she's nowhere to be found so he sits down to have a drink when this pretty young girl sits down next to him.

"Hi handsome, I haven't seen you here before. I'm Fiona and she holds out her hand."

"I'm Daryl and shakes her hand, I'm looking for Kitty, have you seen her?"

"Yeah, she's around here somewhere. I saw her a little while ago, you a friend of hers or something?"

"Yeah, you could say that."

"Well, if I see her I'll be sure to let her know you are looking for her. I go on stage in a few minutes, you should come to see me."

“Oh, you work here?”

“Yeah, I’m one of Kitty’s best dancers, come check me out.”

Daryl hears the music and all the yelling and decides to go check it out, he has a seat up in front by the stage. Fiona smiles at him and starts to give him a lap dance.

Ginger and kitty went down in the cellar to check on the Weasel, when they get down there, he’s still chained to the wheel and blood everywhere so they get closer to get a better look to see where all the blood is coming from.

“My God Kitty, someone found out about the cellar and they cut his tongue out then slit his throat. What do we do now?”

“Let’s just go back in the club and try to conduct business as usual until we can figure this all out.”

Kitty and Ginger go back inside and they see Fiona giving Daryl a lap dance and kissing him, Fiona looks up and sees Kitty and Ginger walk in so she goes back up on stage. Daryl turns around and sees his mom.

Daryl stands up and says, “Mom, where have

you been and hugs her?

We need to talk."

"Okay sweetheart, let's go to my office. So, what were you doing with Fiona?"

"Nothing, she just came up to me and introduced herself and asked me to come to see her dance. What's the big deal. It was just a dance and I haven't been with a woman in a very long time. I was kind of hoping I would get lucky tonight." (he laughs).

"That's not funny. You need to stay away from her, she's bad news."

"If she's bad news then why is she working for you?"

"I just found out and if I fire her it will throw up a red flag and arouse suspicion and I can't take that chance until I figure out what they are after."

"Mom! I can help, I can get close to her and keep an eye out and see what she's up to."

"NO! Absolutely not, I will die if anything happens to you Daryl."

"Nothing is going to happen to me I promise you. I'm very well trained to handle all kinds of situations."

"Alright, but please, please be careful."

"I will mom, don't worry. Now we need to talk about what they are looking for.

Do you have any idea what it is they are after?"

"No, I don't have a clue."

"Well, I have a letter for you to read. It's from Dad, I received it about a year before his death along with this key. I think you should read it."

"Do you suppose that is the key everyone is looking for?"

Kitty takes the letter and as she starts to read tears start to flow down her cheeks.

Dear son,

I want to say first that even tho I'm not your biological father, I've raised you since you were first born so you will always be my son and I've loved you as my own. I'm writing this letter to you in the event of my death. You will be the man of the house when I'm gone so you need to do whatever it takes to make it back home safely. Your mom and sister are going to need you to be there for them and take care of them for me. I've done a lot of things that I am not proud of son, but everything I've done was for both you kids and your mother. This key is very important so please guard it with your life. I need you to go to a safe deposit box at Central Bank in Santa Monica and ask for Mr. Sanchez, he has instructions for you and will be waiting. I have some very incriminating evidence against some very powerful people. The Cartel, the Black Widow also known as Lucinda and I'm so sorry to have to tell you this but your Uncle Vito as well. There will be audio tapes, pictures, videos, documentations with names, dates, places, and numbers. These people will stop at nothing to get their hands on this, they will be coming after both you kids and your mother. If I wind up dead and 6 feet under you can bet your ass it was no accident and that I was murdered. Trust no one, take this evidence and turn it over to the FBI ASAP. Take care of your mother for me and tell her I love her so much. I hope you can find it in your heart to forgive me.

Love you Son,

Dad

Kitty is crying and says, "Wow this is some serious shit, now at least we know what we are dealing with. I need to go find Ginger now."

"Okay. (he gives her a long hug). Things will be okay mom, you will see. I will take care of things, I promise."

"I know you will. Just promise me you will be careful."

"I will mom, now let's go get a drink and relax for a minute and see what Ginger is up to."

"Sounds good, let's go."

Fiona walks up to Ginger and hands her a Jack and coke and puts her arms around her and says, "Hey Miss Ginger, I haven't seen you around much since your accident how are you feeling?"

"I'm doing okay Fiona, thank you for asking."

"So, what did the doctors say, when will your memory come back?"

"They said it would come back in bits and pieces."

"Oh! Well, have you remembered anything at all?"

Ginger downs her jack and coke, "No, no I haven't. I'm not feeling very well right now Fiona I'm kind of light-headed and dizzy can you go and get Kitty for me honey?"

Fiona is just staring and watching Ginger as she stumbles around the room. "Here Miss Ginger let me help you and she puts her arm around her waist to guide her out to a white van with two men waiting for her. It's going to be okay Miss Ginger; these gentlemen will see that you get home safely."

"Okay sweetie, thank you and she passed out in their arms and they put her in the van and drove off."

Fiona goes back inside like nothing has happened and continues to dance up on stage.

Kitty and Daryl walk in and start looking around for Ginger only she's nowhere to be found so they start asking around but no one has seen her.

"I don't like this one-bit Daryl, something bad has happened I can feel it in my blood."

"Mom, we will find her and you will see that everything is okay."

"No, you don't understand son, these people we are dealing with are very dangerous."

"I do understand mom and we are going to find her I promise you."

Fiona is finished dancing for the night and Kitty walks over to her. "Have you seen Ginger tonight?"

"I did briefly before I went up on stage. I know she wasn't feeling too good and said something about going home to lie down. That was the last time I talked to her."

"She wouldn't have left without first telling me. Something's not right here."

"I wish I could be more help, Miss Kitty."

"Yeah, yeah I just bet you do."

"Well, I'm leaving for the night I will see you tomorrow night."

"I will walk you out Fiona," Daryl says.

"Sure, I would like that."

"Sorry about mom, she's just been under a lot of stress lately."

"Did you just say, mom?"

"Yeah, I thought you knew that. Does that make a difference now?"

"No, just surprised, it caught me a little off guard." (she laughs).

"How would you like to go dinner with me and maybe go see a movie?"

"Sure, that sounds like a lot of fun."

"I need to go home and take a shower first, I've been at work all day."

"It's all good, give me your address and I'll pick you up around 7:00."

"Okay, it's 3942 Hartford Street. I'll see you then."

"Yes, you will for sure."

Fiona goes home to get ready and makes a call.

"Hello!"

"Hey pops, the merchandise is on its way."

"Good job."

"Yea, well I almost got busted by Kitty and that son of hers."

"Her son?"

"Yes, I will tell you about it later but right now I have to get ready for my date."

"A date! Who with?"

"Daryl, Kitty's son."

"I don't think that's such a good ideal Fiona."

"Don't worry Papi, I'll be alright."

"Call me when you get home."

"Alright, I'll talk to you later. Love you."

"Love you too Hija."

Daryl shows up right on time wearing a pair of nice black tight-fitting jeans with a red silk shirt unbuttoned to the third button exposing his chest with a gold chain around his neck and his gold Rolex with a nice gold ring on his finger.

He watches Fiona as she comes down the

stairs in her tight black mini skirt with a blue half shirt barely coming down to cover her breasts with the words "Rise to the Occasion," on the front and a black leather jacket showing off her tattoo around her belly button of a spider web with a piercing in the middle and her 4" red heels.

"Wow, you look beautiful" and hands her a bouquet of flowers and kisses her on the cheek and opens the car door for her.

"Thank you. Damn this is one nice looking ride."

"Glad you like it, I just bought it today."

"So I hope you like Italian. I thought we could go to Lugi's fine dining up on Watson Road."

"That sounds really great."

They get to the restaurant but the wait is about 30 minutes so they sit at the bar and have a few drinks until their table is ready. They were seated at 7:45. Fiona ordered the Beef Brasato with Pappardelle and Mint and Daryl ordered Tuscan Tomato Bread Soup with Steamed Mussels and he ordered a bottle of their best wine.

"Wow this is amazing, thank you for inviting me to dinner."

"You're welcome and I am glad you accepted the invitation."

"How would you like to go to the Drive Inn and see Silver Streak? There's a double feature but I don't remember the other movie that is playing."

"That's cool and sounds like fun. I'm down. I don't think I've ever been to a Drive Inn before."

"Really! Well, you will love it, I promise you that."

"I can't wait. What exactly is a Drive Inn?"

"You're serious, aren't you? Well, you are in for a treat my dear."

They pull up to the I-44 Drive Inn and park and Daryl grabs the speaker and attaches it to the door of the car.

"What are you doing Daryl?"

"Oh, well this is how we hear the movie."

"Wow, an outside movie theatre, how exciting."

"Glad you think so. Now for a special treat."

He reaches into his cooler in the back seat and pulls out a bottle of wine and two chilled glasses and some chocolate-covered strawberries.

"Well look at you Mr. romantic, coming all prepared. Impressive!"

"Well, of course, only the best for such a beautiful woman."

"Aww thank you Daryl for making this such a wonderful evening." (She kisses him on the cheek). She moves closer to him and they cuddle and watch both of the movies. The movies were over at 12:30 a.m. and now they are on their way home.

Daryl pulls up to Fiona's house and he gets out and opens her car door for her and walks her up to her front door.

"Thank you Daryl, I had an amazing time tonight. Would you like to come in for a while and maybe have another drink with me?"

"No, I'd better not but thank you, maybe some other night." He kisses her good night.

"Awww, please just one last one then we can call it a night. What harm can that do?"

"Okay, just one then I have to go."

They go into the living room and Fiona tells Daryl to have a seat.

"I will be back in a minute, I'm going to go and get comfortable, do you mind?" "No, not at all, knock yourself out."

Ten minutes later Fiona comes out in a black

lace see-through negligee showing every inch and curve of her body with her nipples hard as can be and pointy.

"Wow! Now that does look comfortable."

She pours them a drink and puts some kind of drug in his drink then starts to massage his shoulders. "You're so tense, loosen up a little."

"If I didn't know better, I'd think you were trying to seduce me." (He laughs).

Fiona walks around the couch and sits on his lap and starts to kiss him." Would that be a bad thing?"

"No, but let's not start anything we can't finish, as much as I would love to, I really do need to go, maybe we can pick up where we left off on another night."

"Okay, I'm gonna hold you to that, you haven't touched your drink, don't you want to finish it before you go?"

"No, I better not, I've already had too much." He gives her a long kiss, "I will see you later beautiful."

"Bye for now."

Daryl takes off in his convertible and heads

home. (Phone rings).

"Hello." Fiona says.

"I'm sorry, he's gonna be a bigger challenge than I thought. I've got it under control."

"Yes, I understand."

"Good night." She hangs up the phone and throws it across the room yelling and cussing and pulling at her hair.

CHAPTER 13

It's 6:00 a.m. and I wake up to the smell of freshly brewed coffee, I walk into the kitchen and don't see anyone so I pour myself a cup of hot coffee then walk into the living room and still don't see anyone, I decide to go and sit on the front balcony and low and behold Daryl and mom are having their morning coffee. As I go through the entrance of the balcony the breeze of the cool crisp air hits me in the face and is so refreshing. "Ahh, there you both are I was wondering where everyone was at."

"I was just telling mom that I will be heading out this morning to go to Santa Monica and I will be back at the end of the week if everything goes as planned."

"Great! I'm coming with you; I just need to go pack a few things."

"No, Shiloh you need to stay here with mom and take care of her. I can handle this by myself."

"I'm okay Daryl, I can take care of myself and I don't need a babysitter. You both need to go and get this so-called evidence and turn it over to the FBI so we can get this all behind us and start living our normal lives again. Now I need to go and find Ginger,

I don't believe anything that Bitch Fiona says."

"Wait a minute now Mom, you don't know that Fiona had anything to do with Ginger disappearing."

Kitty and Shiloh both turn and look at Daryl. "You dirty dog you," says Shiloh. "You did the deed didn't you?"

"I thought I told you not to get involved with her Daryl, she is bad news, how could you?"

"Now wait a minute both of you. I haven't done the deed with anyone. We went out to eat then to see a movie at the Drive Inn that's it, nothing happened."

"If you say so little brother."

"Yes, I say so now let's drop it."

Shiloh jumps up and runs to the bathroom and starts throwing up. When she comes back to the balcony everyone is asking her if she is okay and if she needs to go to the doctor.

"No! I'm fine, it's probably something I ate and it just upset my stomach a little, that's all, I will be fine."

Shiloh looks down at the street and says, "Damn whose fine ass car is that and why is it parked in this neighborhood?"

"You mean that 1974 Eldorado?" Daryl says.

"Yeah."

"It belongs to me, I just bought it yesterday morning."

"Sweet, are we driving that to Santa Monica?"

"Yup."

"Mom you take good care of my Mustang while I'm gone and I don't want a scratch on it, I mean it."

"Don't worry honey, I will take good care of it for you."

"Okay, well I got to go pack a few things for the road, now you are sure that you will be okay till we get back?"

"Yes, I'm sure."

Ace comes downstairs and sees Shiloh's packed bag. "Are you going somewhere?"

"Yes, I have a friend that is very ill and needs me to come stay with her for a few days."

"Oh, well I hope it's not too serious. Is there anything I can do to help?" "No, but thanks for the offer."

Darryl comes running down the stairs. "Okay big sis ready to hit the road so we can beat the rush hour traffic."

"It's Sunday, there shouldn't be any rush hour

traffic today."

"Oh yeah, your right." (he laughs)

"I thought you said you were going to help a sick friend?" Ace says.

"I am, Daryl is driving me."

"Uh-huh!"

"Okay, well we have to hit the highway now Mom, love you, I will call you later and I will talk to you later Ace."

"Yes, you will." Ace watches them pull away then he turns to Kitty and says, "Okay Kitty level with me, where are they going?"

"She told you to go help a sick friend."

"That's your story?"

"Yes, that's my story and I'm sticking to it. Are you calling my daughter a liar?" "No, not at all, I'm just not so sure she is being completely honest with me."

"Well Ace, that is something you need to take up with Shiloh. I have to go and get dressed now, I have something that I need to take care of today, so if you'll excuse me."

"Yes, of course."

Kitty gets out of the shower and puts on her

blue jean hip-hugger bell-bottoms with a pink half-shirt with rhinestones in the shape of a heart and pink running shoes. She notices Ace is gone so she calls Ginger but no answer, she then calls Dillan, also no answer. She feeds her cats and takes care of them, then she grabs Shiloh's keys to the Mustang and runs out of the house with Cochise and Nikita right behind her. They all three jumps into the car and she guns it and takes off.

"Daryl, can you pull over for a minute? I think I'm about to be sick again."

"Yeah sure, what's going on with you Shiloh? Are you coming down with the flu or something?"

"I don't know, (she throws up) it just started yesterday morning."

"Well, we are in Amarillo right now, why don't we get a couple of rooms, and you can take a nice long hot bubble bath and relax, get some rest, and order in some food and we can get an early start in the morning."

"That sounds like a really great idea, I'm exhausted."

"I will call mom while you're taking your bath and fill her in on our progress sonfar."

"Okay bro, sounds good."

Daryl calls home but there's no answer so he pages Kitty. Kitty receives the page so she stops at a payphone to call the number. (Phone rings). "Hello! Hey mom, just checking in with you." Daryl proceeds to tell his mom where they are and what's been happening with Shiloh and how they stopped at a Motel for the night so she could get some rest and they will leave first thing in the morning. "How's Ginger?"

"I'm glad you are taking care of your sister. As for Ginger I still haven't heard from her or Dillan. I went to her house and she wasn't home. I have no clue where she can be and I'm worried to death about her."

"Well, we should be home by the end of the week and we will find her. I'll call you later mom. Love you and don't go and do anything crazy."

"Love you too, please be careful. Oh, one more thing, I haven't seen Ace around since you guys left."

"Really! Well, that's interesting. Okay mom, thanks. I will talk to you later." (They disconnect).

Shiloh is taking a bath and listening to her music and having a glass of wine when her bedroom door opens slowly and there's a dark figure rummaging through her things then he looks in the bathroom and watches her for a while. She calls out, is someone there, "Daryl is that you?" She listens for a minute but doesn't hear anything so she continues with her bath. She hears a noise again so she gets out of the bathtub and grabs her gun and tip toes into the other room to see who is there. She catches a glimpse of someone by the balcony and she fires her gun but he jumps off the balcony and takes off running. Daryl hears the gun and runs to her room to see if she is okay.

They call the police but when they arrive there really wasn't much to tell she couldn't see his face and doesn't even know if it was a man or woman. The security system is down in the motel so they can't check the footage. There's a store across the street that might have a security system that might be able to show the perpetrator. The detective asks if they know of any reason why someone would be in her room but Daryl and Shiloh say they have no idea why anyone would come into her room. "I'm going to stay in your room tonight Shiloh in case he comes back. Someone must have followed us when we left the house. I doubt this is any coincidence."

"You're right Daryl this is no coincidence. Good thing I had my gun in the bathroom drawer." Daryl looks around the room and sees a few drops of blood. He asks Shiloh if she by any chance cut herself but her reply was no. "Well, I think you may have hit him when you shot at him because there's blood on the balcony. Mom did tell me something quite interesting when I talked to her. She said she hasn't seen Ace since we left. You don't suppose he followed us here and that was him in the room, do you?"

"Huh, I don't know but anything is possible. He claims he loves me and I'm his life and he can't live without me so why would he be doing this."

"People do a lot of stupid shit out of greed Shiloh, that doesn't mean he doesn't love you; it just means he got caught up in something over his head."

"Yeah, I guess you're right. Well, I'm ready to turn in now so we can get up early and get on the road."

"Not before you eat, I ordered a pizza and it should be here in a few minutes. I promised mom that I would take care of you, now what kind of brother would I be if I let my sister go to bed hungry."

"Okay, thanks, I am kind of hungry." (she laughs).

(Knock at door). Daryl hides behind the door with his gun drawn and Shiloh peeks through the peephole and unlocks the door. It's the pizza guy. Daryl pays the guy then shuts the door.

"Oh my God this pizza is so good, I didn't think I was that hungry. I'm going to get me a beer do you want one?"

"Does a wild bear shit in the woods?" (They both laugh)

Shiloh gets them both a beer. They finish their beer and pizza and go to bed so they can get a fresh start in the morning.

Daryl slept on the rollaway bed with his shotgun next to him and Shiloh slept in the bed with her .45 under her pillow. They were going to be ready for the next time if anything decides to pop off. While they slept there was a dark figure across the street in the shadows watching the motel just waiting for them to leave.

The alarm went off at 5:00 a.m. so Shiloh and Daryl went downstairs to the hotel lobby and got a cup of coffee and to check out. The Clerk at the front desk gave him a refund on his room since they both stayed in the same room. They walk out to the car but Daryl holds Shiloh back and tells her not to go near the car, something doesn't seem right. He inspects the car and sees a wire sticking out under the car so he follows the wire and it's wired to blow when he turns on the ignition. Daryl was trained in explosives when he was in the Military so he very carefully disarmed the bomb but they did not want to get the police involved since they had to get to Santa Monica real quick and back home.

"Well, Shiloh if it is Ace behind this and we don't know this for sure but someone is out for blood they don't want us making it back alive."

"I can't imagine him trying to kill me though."

"Well, only time will tell. We better hurry. We should be there by 10:00 p.m. tonight if we take shifts driving then we will stay in a hotel or motel and get to the bank first thing in the morning to see Mr. Sanchez. I think whoever is behind this probably doesn't want us dead yet until we get all the evidence from the bank first then we probably should really watch our backs. It's probably going to be hell getting back to St. Louis."

"Yes, I agree and I can't wait for this all to be over with so we can get back to our normal lives. I'm worried about mom though, especially since she is there all by herself. I think maybe I should call the detective and have him keep an eye on her for us until we get back."

"I think that would be a good idea, Shiloh, I will pull over at the next gas station and you can call him while I fill the car up."

They stopped at a small gas station in Arizona. Not much there but a lot of cattle and some rattlesnakes and the good ole Grand Canyon of course. Shiloh goes over to the payphone and dials detective Lorenzo.

"Hello!"

"Eddie, this is Shiloh I have a favor to ask of you."

"Where have you been? I've been calling you and I went by your house and it's all dark and no one is home which is unusual for your house. Now, what is going on?"

"I know and I am sorry. Daryl and I had to take a trip and will be back by the end of the week. I need you to look after my mom for me, I'm worried about her. Ginger has been missing for a few days and no one has seen or heard from her and mom is going crazy and I don't want her to do anything stupid or get into trouble. I will explain everything when I get back, I promise. I believe she might be in danger; I don't have time to explain right now just please take care of her till I get back. I will make it up to you I promise and Eddie, thank you."

"Okay, I can see that you are not going to tell me anything right now but the minute you get back you have some explaining to do. I will put an officer on your mom to keep her safe. I don't like this one-bit Shiloh and I am not very happy about this."

"I know, I know but I promise the minute I get back I will tell you everything." (She hangs up the phone).

"Hello, Shiloh, hello, hello. Damn, she hung up the phone."

"Well, I got a hold of Eddie and he was furious with me but said he would put an officer on mom to keep her safe and I promised to tell him everything when we get back."

"Okay good. So, what's up with you and this detective? Are you two an item now? Sure, sounds like it."

"No, nothing like that, we went out a few times, that's it nothing serious. Not yet anyway."

"Okay if you say so. I picked up a couple of sodas and sandwiches for us for the road."

"Good, I'm starved. I need to go use the bathroom before we get back on the road and I'm feeling kind of sick again. I hate this."

"When we get back you are going to go to the VA to get checked out."

"Yes, Sir."

"I mean it, Shiloh."

"Okay, Okay."

As Daryl and Shiloh continue their trip to Santa Monica Kitty continues her search for Ginger. She goes back to the club where Ginger was last seen and starts asking around if anyone had seen her leave but no one is talking. It's like they are afraid of something or someone. Kitty went to find Fiona since she seems to be the last one to see her, only Fiona called in tonight. Kitty finds that very strange since Fiona has never called in the whole time she has worked here. Kitty goes into her office and starts watching the security footage of that night.

"Okay Ginger, what happened? I'm going to find you just hang tight and whoever is behind you disappearing is going to regret the day they were born; I promise you that. There has to be something here that I'm missing."

Big Al comes in to see Kitty," alright Miss Kitty we've closed down for the night and everything is cleaned and everyone has gone home for the night. I'm going to lock up and take off. Do you need me to hang around till you leave? I don't want you disappearing too."

"No, but thanks. I will be okay; I have Cochise and Nikita here with me. I'll be leaving here shortly."

"Alright, well then if there's not anything else I will see you tomorrow."

"Yes, well good night Big Al."

Kitty continues to watch the footage, after hours of reviewing she notices someone lurking in the shadows. She sees the side door open and they seem to have a hold of Ginger's arm, then she sees the van and 2 men walk up to the side door, the camera just went fuzzy and blank. Damn someone didn't switch out the VCR tape and it ran out of video.

All of a sudden Kitty hears a door open and

footsteps coming down the hall. She grabs a baseball bat and her pepper spray then turns off the office light. When the footsteps stop at the office door Kitty jumps out and screams, "You messed with the wrong Bitch," then she smacks him in the legs with the bat and sprays him in the eyes with her pepper spray, and Cochise and Nikita have him by the legs and growling.

"Detective? Why are you sneaking around my bar?"

"Do you mind getting up off me? My eyes are burning, do you have an eyewash station around here?"

"How was I supposed to know it was you detective? You could have identified yourself first. I was protecting myself. The eyewash station is over here in the corner. Let me take a look. Now, what in the hell are you doing here?"

"Damn, I think your daughter underestimates your ability to take care of yourself." "What are you talking about? What about Shiloh?"

"She said something about Ginger missing. I came by to help find her."

They both go back into Kitty's office and she

shows him the footage of the night when Ginger disappeared.

"I'm going to take this tape down to the precinct and put it into evidence and have it examined to see what we can find out. Don't worry we will find her. I will walk you out and you need to go straight home and get some rest and leave it to me."

CHAPTER 14

Daryl and Shiloh are driving down the 405 interstates when an emergency broadcast comes over the radio ordering everyone to evacuate the area, the forest fires are spreading like wildfires.

"Did you hear that Daryl, now what? There's no other way to get there."

"We are almost there Shiloh. He pulls the car over and goes to the trunk of the car and pulls out two yellow suits and hands her one."

"What the hell is this, Daryl?"

"It's a fire suit for your protection."

She puts it on, "damn I look like big bird."

"Who cares what you look like you're not going to a fashion show. We are going to drive through this, it's the only way we have no other choice."

"No, it's too risky and dangerous."

"You really underestimate your little brother." (He laughs). "Trust me on this, will you? Don't forget I was in Nam and I've been through worse situations than a forest fire. We can and will get through this, understand me?"

"Alright little brother, let's do it."

Daryl puts the top up on his car and they both have on their yellow fire protectant suits so he starts to drive through the grey smoke and heat, up ahead you can see the yellow and red flames with the firefighters working hard to control it and put it out. A tree falls but misses the car, the debris and sparks are flying everywhere. Shiloh closes her eyes and starts praying they make it out alive, when she opens her eyes back up, they are driving out of the fire. As soon as they are far enough away, they pull over and get out of the car and grab their things and begin to run when the car explodes throwing them in the air coming down hard on the pavement knocking the wind out of them.

"Oh my God, Daryl, your beautiful car."

"It's ok, easy come easy go I had insurance. I will just buy myself another one when we get back to St. Louis, but right now we need to get a hotel room and get cleaned up, get some food and rest then go to the bank in the morning and finish taking care of business so we can hurry and get back home. We can just fly into St. Louis so we will be back sooner than expected then."

They were both sitting on the pavement when

a squad car approached them to find out what had happened and if everyone was okay. The officer called an ambulance to check them out but they refused to go to the hospital so the officer gave them a ride to the nearest enterprise car rental.

"Thank you so much officer for the ride," Shiloh says.

"No problem ma'am, you folks be careful now.:

"We will and thank you again."

They rented a car and got on the I-10 going into Santa Monica. When they got there all the hotels were booked up and the last hotel they found had only one room left so they had to share the room. The rustic hotel was a rundown hole in the wall with one bed and a couch. The TV didn't work and the bathroom only had cold water for them to take their shower, the refrigerator looked like it hadn't been cleaned in six months, there were holes in the wall. The walls were paper thin that you could hear everything that went on in the next room.

"Damn, if it wasn't for bad luck, we'd have no luck at all," Shiloh says.

"Well, you get cleaned up first Shiloh and I'll go find us something to eat. I'll be back in a bit."

Daryl goes to the front desk to see if any places are open where they could get something to eat. The clerk tells him about three miles east there's an all-night diner.

Daryl drives and sees a neon sign that says "Gypsy's Diner." He walks into the diner and sees only 5 blue bar stools that had rips and tears on them and 5 red tables with red and blue walls with different colored flowers painted on them in red, blue, yellow, orange, and green. The staff was dressed in long multi-colored skirts with brown boots and white ruffled blouses that barely covered their midriff. They were wearing multi-colored scarfs on their head with long earrings and a ring on each finger with bracelets on each wrist.

"Hi darling, I'm Gypsy what can I get for you tonight?" Gypsy is the owner and is 5'10 with blonde hair and blue eyes, 210 pounds with a heavy southern accent.

"Hi, I'd like two cheeseburgers, one with crispy fries and one with onion rings with two Dr. Peppers to go."

"Coming right up sweet thing."

As Daryl waits for his food a woman walks up

to him, "I'm sensing trouble coming your way and I see Death everywhere, come with me and I will tell you what your future holds for you."

Daryl looks at her in amusement. "I'm sorry lady I'm not in the mood maybe some other time."

"Suit yourself but evil is lurking around the corner."

"Here's your order Sir, that will be $12.95."

He hands her $20 and tells her to keep the change.

"Thank you, young man, and may God be with you."

Daryl gets back to the hotel and Shiloh is out of the shower and in bed. "I got you a cheeseburger and onion rings with a Dr. Pepper. "

Thanks, Shiloh begins to eat her cheeseburger and it's dripping with grease and pink inside and her onion rings are burnt and her soda is flat. "Damn, this is the worst food I've ever tasted and she throws it in the garbage. I'm tired, I'm going to sleep now. It was a really rough day and night."

"Okay Shiloh, I'm going to finish eating and take my shower then hit the sack.

Good luck there is no hot water. I had to take a

cold shower."

"That's just great. Okay, see you in the morning."

As Daryl and Shiloh try to sleep all they can hear is the banging of a headboard against their wall and a lot of moaning making it hard for them to sleep. Shiloh bangs her fist on the wall and yells at them to quiet down and be more considerate of the other people staying there, but they ignore her and keep at it. She gets up and gets dressed and gets her gun.

"Where do you think you're going"

"I'm going next door and by God when I'm done with them, they will wish they were never born. I've had it."

"No, we don't need any trouble, just go back to bed."

"Hell no, I can't sleep with all that racket going on over there. She goes next door and bangs on their door with the butt of her gun. The man opens the door, "Yeah what the hell do you want?" I'm kind of busy here."

She kicks in the door and puts her gun to his head and says, "Now I'm only going to say this once if you don't quiet the fuck down so I can sleep I'm going to blow your brains out and if you call the cops when I go back to my room I will hunt you down like the dog you are, do I make myself clear?"

"Yes, yes ma'am. We are sorry and will be quieter."

"That's better, now good night."

"Was that really necessary Shiloh?"

"Yes dammit, I'm fucking tired and need sleep. I was just almost killed in a forest fire, your car exploded, we are staying in a piece of a shit hotel with no hot water and no TV and the food was disgusting. Now I'm going back to bed. Good night."

"Okay, see you in the morning."

The next morning their alarm went off at 6:00 a.m., they got dressed and went downstairs to check out. The clerk told them that the people in the next room checked out last night because there was a crazy lady with a gun that busted down their door and threatened to blow their brains out and asked if we heard or saw anything. They were afraid for their life.

"No, that's terrible we didn't hear anything. I was so tired I went to sleep right away and didn't hear a thing. Well, here are our keys, we will be leaving now."

"I need coffee, Daryl. We need to find a place to stop."

"There's a Burger Chef a few miles up the road we can stop there and get breakfast and some coffee."

"That sounds fabulous. We need to call and check on mom when we stop."

Kitty is sitting in the living room with Sassy on her lap and Cochise and Nikita on each side of her. As she watches the morning news, she sees the forest fire on the news, she starts to panic because that's the only way to go to get to Santa Monica. As she continues to watch she hears that a young girl and a young man whose names they don't know barely escaped death when their car exploded after driving through the fire. The phone rings and she jumps up off the couch and runs to the phone and trips over one of the dog's toys and falls on the floor so she grabs the phone cord and pulls the phone down to her.

"Hello! Shiloh, is that you?"

"Mom, are you ok, what's going on? You sound out of breath."

"Nothing, I'm fine, I just saw the news. Are you

ok?"

"Yes, we are good mom, you don't need to worry. We just stopped at Burger Chef for breakfast then we are on our way to the bank. I just wanted to check in with you and let you know what's going on."

"I am gonna worry to death until you and your brother are home safe and sound."

"Don't worry mom we will be okay. So, what's the news on Ginger."

"Still no news but there was some footage captured on one of the tapes so Detective Lorenzo took it downtown to examine it."

"Well, that's great news mom. Well, I have to go now but I will call again later on."

"Okay, until then be safe."

"We will mom and you do the same, bye for now."

CHAPTER 15

Shiloh and Darryl finish their breakfast and head on over to the bank to see Mr. Sanchez. They walked into the bank and it was like walking into a palace. It is a huge beautiful bank with high cathedral ceilings with beautiful crystal chandeliers hanging down and a round staircase going upstairs to where all the loan officers and accounting offices are. There were at least 12 tellers behind gold-plated glass windows and a five-car drive-thru. There was a doorman that greeted everyone and answers questions to make things move more quickly. There were cameras at every door and teller station and in every corner and outside facing the front and on every drive-thru station as well.

"Wow this is amazing, I have never seen a bank like this before," Shiloh says to the doorman.

"How may I help you today Ma'am?"

"We are here to see Mr. Sanchez."

"May I have your name?"

"Yes, tell him Shiloh and Daryl Russo are here to see him."

The doorman has an earbud in his ear and lets

Mr. Sanchez know he has guests.

"He will be right down, you may have a seat right inside." Mr. Sanchez greets them and shakes their hand.

"I am sure you are aware of our father's death, he said for us to speak to you specifically and you would explain things to us and let us know what is going on."

"Yes, and I am very sorry for your loss, please follow me. I have known your father since we were kids. He was a very good man. He takes them to where the safety deposit boxes are kept. Have a seat. We will be able to talk privately here. Your father has been coming here for years and putting money back for his family. He didn't believe in putting it in an account. He was involved in some serious things that weren't so legal and got in some deep trouble with the government and the mafia. They were both after him so he came to me for help. "

"What kind of trouble and what about his brother?"

"Well his brother couldn't be trusted either he was in pretty deep himself running guns and drugs across the border and got involved with the cartel and the black widow. The black widow has Vito under her claws pretty good and she ordered a hit on your father but here's the kicker: your Uncle Vito was the hitman. Your father knew he was about to die so he came to me and wanted me to tell you everything that I know and make sure that you kids and your Mother were taken care of. The things that you are going to see will put these people away for good including your Uncle Vito. You have to be prepared to put your uncle Vito behind bars. He won't hesitate to kill you both and your mother. Here is a card with the name of an FBI agent that you should contact and turn over this evidence to so you can put all this behind you and get on with your lives or else you will always be looking over your shoulder. Do you understand how serious this is?"

"Yes, we understand."

"I will leave you so you can go through the things in the safety deposit box. Let me know if you need anything. Take all the time you need, no need to rush."

"Thank you, Mr. Sanchez."

Daryl opens the safety deposit box and starts pulling everything out. "Oh my God, would you look at all this money Shiloh."

"Damn, how do we know that's not blood money."

"We don't. Let's not think about that right now."

Daryl pulls out a small blue velvet bag and empties it." Oh shit, would you look at this, there must be millions here in diamonds." He starts looking at all the tapes and documents in front of him and a letter. Daryl starts to read the letter.

My dearest children and wife, Mr. Sanchez is my longtime friend and I trust that he told you how important it is that you get this over to the FBI as quickly as you can. From here you need to go to Washington DC and get a hold of the agent on the card that was handed to you by Mr. Sanchez. They will take care of everything. As far as the money and diamonds go that is for you kids and your mother to start a new life wherever you want to go and never have to worry about a thing. I've saved it over the years so you could have a better future and not have to struggle and worry about anything. I know I have hurt you both and your mother and this won't begin to make up for it but I hope someday you will learn to forgive me. When you leave the bank be careful there are eyes everywhere and they are watching you and will stop at nothing short of killing you to get their hands on this evidence because it will put a lot of people away for a very long time. Ama tuo padre. (Love your father).

Shiloh and Daryl start putting everything into the duffel bag then they buzz for Mr. Sanchez to come back in.

"We want to thank you Mr. Sanchez for everything you have done for our family. We will be going now; do we need to sign any papers that we cleaned out the deposit box."

"Yes, I do need a few signatures then you may go."

Daryl and Shiloh sign the necessary papers then they turn around to see four masked gunmen enter the bank and tell everyone to get down on the floor.

"Damn is there any other way out of here?" Shiloh asks.

"Yes, follow me, I designed this building myself. There are several ways out we will go to the underground tunnel."

"You must have anticipated trouble."

"Trouble is always expected when dealing with banks. This is one of the largest banks in the state of California. We deal with millions and millions of dollars each day."

"Shouldn't you call the police?"

"No, there's no need. I have a built-in face recognition on the cameras which means no one is allowed into the bank with any face coverings and if anyone doesn't abide by it an alert goes straight to the PD or if anyone carries weapons the sensors also pick up on it and the place will be surrounded within a matter of minutes."

"Looks like you thought of everything."

"Well, this is the end of the line for me kids. Just follow this to the end and it will take you to the subway station."

"Wait you're not going back in there are you?"

"Yes, I have to. I can't just abandon my team like that. You kids be careful out there."

"You're a good man Mr. Sanchez, thank you."

Sanchez turns around and jogs back to the bank before anyone notices he's not there. As he is coming out of the bathroom one of the gunmen comes up to him from behind and puts a gun to his head and says, “Where are they?”

“Gone.”

“What do you mean gone?”

“Exactly what I said, Gone. Do I need to spell it out for you? Now you better get that gun out of my head unless you plan on using it.” As he turns around, he says, “You didn’t follow the plan, you morons. They are probably at the subway by now. I put a tracking device in their bag now you fools better go get them and shoot to kill we can’t afford any loose ends.”

“Yes Sir, we got this.”

The gunman runs down the stairs where the other gunmen are and says, “They are gone, let’s go. Everyone stay down for 30 minutes or we will blow this place sky high.”

Everyone did as they were told and as the gunmen ran out of the bank to jump in their car it was gone.

“Where’s the fucking car, Lenny?”

“I only left it for a quick minute so I could go take a piss.”

“You had to take a piss during a job you idiot and you left the fucking key in the car and running.

You are a get-a-getaway driver. That means you stay in the fucking car and wait for us to come out then you drive like a bat out of hell. They hear police sirens getting closer and closer, Okay now what."

"Look across the street there's a bike stand, I say let's go jack them and get the hell out of dodge."

"Squiggy starts laughing, you can't be serious. That's just genius, a getaway on bicycles."

"Well, you got a better idea? The cops are getting close and I'm not sticking around, you hear me!!"

"Okay let's do this."

The gunmen get to the subway but Daryl and Shiloh are nowhere to be found.

Damn, where are they? Pull out the tracker you idiot.

"Oh yeah, I forgot."

Daryl and Shiloh found a hotel along the ocean so they could shower, eat and get some rest. They fell asleep but Shiloh was awakened by Daryl. He was yelling and speaking in a language she couldn't understand and was breaking out in a sweat. When she tried to wake him, he grabbed her by the throat and started squeezing and choking her. Shiloh tried her best to get out of his hold but he was too strong so she grabbed the lamp and hit him. He snapped out of it and came to and Shiloh was massaging her neck.

"Oh my God Shiloh, Did I do that? I am so sorry."

"You tried to kill me, that must have been some nightmare."

"Ever since I got out of the war, I can't shake these nightmares. I don't expect you to understand unless you've been through it or lived it. It was a horrible and frightening experience that I wouldn't wish on anyone. It really messes with your head. Images that you will never forget."

"I'm sorry you had to go through that and when this is all over, we will get you some help in dealing with all of this on how to cope. I think we better get ready to roll out now."

The gunmen get to the hotel and stake it out.

It's four in the morning and not a sole is up. The stars are shining bright and all you can hear are the sounds of the waves from the ocean.

"It's so peaceful here. I'm going to put on some coffee before we leave."

"That sounds great Shiloh, I could use some

right about now."

Daryl is in the bathroom getting dressed and Shiloh is already dressed in a red halter top with a blue scarf around her neck to hide the marks on her neck, a black hat turned to the side and a pair of black cargo pants with her running shoes on in case she needs to take off in a hurry. Daryl comes out of the bathroom wearing a pair of camouflage cargo pants and a green army t-shirt to match with a green beret on and his combat boots. He puts on his utility belt with his knives, guns, and grenades. He hands Shiloh a utility belt and she puts her knife, taser gun, pepper spray, and guns in the holster. They put on their backpacks and head for the door.

"Are you ready for this Shiloh?"

"Yes, let's do it."

Daryl peeks out the curtain first to see if anyone is out there watching the hotel. "I think we have company Shiloh. We have to move now."

Daryl and Shiloh climb out the bathroom window and sneak around to their car as the men surround the hotel and bust in the door. Daryl throws a hand grenade into their car and there's a big explosion. The guys come running out of the room and see their car up in flames.

"Damn there goes our car. It's OK we will just have to hot-wire another one." They see a nice red firebird at the far end of the parking lot. Well look what we have here, One Eye points his rifle at two young teens in the backseat making out. "Do your parents know what you are doing out here?"

"No Sir," says the girl.

"Well today is your lucky day get out of the car and I won't tell them. We need to borrow your car for an emergency."

"My dad will kill me if I don't return his car home." Says the boy.

"Well, I will kill you if you don't hand over the keys. I'll tell you what, you can have my car in its place and he points across the parking lot to the burning car."

The boy gets out of the car and hands him the keys then the kids take off running.

The men jump in the car and chase after Shiloh and Daryl.

As the chase goes on, they are going through town and people are walking and the traffic is crazy and the men are shooting at Shiloh and Daryl. The cars are all honking and the people are running to get out of the way of the fire. Daryl is driving and Shiloh is shooting back at them. Shiloh managed to hit the driver and he lost control of the car. The men saw that they were heading for the gas station so they jumped out of the car but the driver didn't make it before the car hit the tanks and exploded.

"Ooh Wee, would you look at that Shiloh, Nice. I see you haven't lost your skills."

Daryl pulls over to the side of the road to watch the gas station up in flames and make sure no one walks away. "Well look at that Shiloh, looks like a few got away with an inch of their life. Lucky bastards". Daryl pulls out his M-40 rifle and lines it up at one of the men and shoots him right square in the forehead. The other two men take cover but have no idea where the shot came from. There's so much commotion going on that

Daryl doesn't have another good shot and doesn't want to risk hurting any innocent bystanders. The Police, ambulance, and fire trucks arrive on the scene so Daryl and Shiloh take off and the other two men managed to elude the police.

CHAPTER 16

Kitty arrives back home with her two K-9's and detective Lorenzo is waiting on her front porch.

"Detective, have you found out anything on Ginger yet?"

"We need to talk upstairs Kitty."

"Okay, I will put on a pot of coffee."

"That sounds good, I'm going to use the bathroom if that's okay with you." "Sure, go right ahead detective."

Detective Lorenzo starts looking around upstairs and in all the other rooms while Kitty is in the kitchen making coffee and a snack. He goes into Kitty's room and sees all this surveillance equipment hooked up and realizes it's hooked up to Vito's apartment.

"Detective are you okay?"

Kitty doesn't hear a response so she goes looking for him. She opens her bedroom door and sees him going through her equipment.

"Have you found what you are looking for? This doesn't look like the bathroom; did you get lost? What gives you the right to go snooping through my things and without a warrant?"

"Kitty, I'm just looking for clues that might lead us to Ginger."

"So, you think I might have had something to do with my best friend disappearing?"

"No, not at all, you might have something and not even know it. I'm trained to find things like that to lead us in the right direction. Where did you get all of this equipment? It's police issued, you didn't...."

"Kitty cuts him off, don't even say it, I did not steal any of it. I borrowed it from a friend".

"I can go get a warrant if you wish."

"Well, it will be all gone by the time you get back with the warrant then you will have nothing."

"Kitty work with me on this so we can find Ginger." "Okay, what do you need me to do."

"I need to go through these tapes to see if there is something that might lead us to Ginger. In the meantime, I think we need to put you into protective custody."

"Like hell you say, I'm not going anywhere. I have responsibilities."

"I have a responsibility to keep you alive and safe. We will discuss this after I listen to the tapes.

Do you mind if I get a cup of coffee now?"

"Sure, I will bring you one. Would you like sugar or cream?"

"No, just black, thanks. "

"I also made some horderves."

"That sounds great."

While Kitty is in the kitchen getting coffee and horderves the detective is listening to the tapes to see if he can find any clues. The doorbell rings

"Are you expecting company?"

"No".

Detective Lorenzo pulls out his gun and watches carefully as Kitty answers the door.

"Mrs. Marmalade, what can I do for you?"

"Well, I noticed that you have been having the police here a lot lately and I was wondering if everything was okay. There have just been all kinds of activity going on over here it seems."

"I appreciate your concern Mrs. Marmalade but everything is fine. My daughter is just seeing this detective so that's why you have been seeing the police here."

"Are you sure? It just seems like a lot more if you ask me."

"Well, I'm not asking, now if you will excuse me, I was in the middle of something.

Have a great day". Kitty shuts the door.

Mrs. Marmalade knocks on the door again and yells for Kitty.

Kitty ignores the door and goes back upstairs.

"Who was that?"

"It was my nosey neighbor Mrs. Marmalade. She's the neighborhood watch." "That's great, maybe she has seen something. I will go see her after we are done here. I need to finish listening to these tapes first. Wow, this is some serious shit. With your permission, I would like to take this into evidence."

"Only the tapes, not the equipment."

Okay deal. Now let's talk about you.

"There's nothing to talk about."

"Oh yes there is, your safety. Since you won't let me put you into PC then I will have an officer assigned to you."

"There's no need for that, I can take care of myself you saw that first hand."

"I can just detain you for up to 24 hours if I have to, it's up to you. Now, do you want to cooperate with me and let me protect you?"

"Okay fine."

"Now which house does your neighbor Mrs. Marmalade live in?"

She lives across the street 3rd house down with the blue shutters and small garden in front.

Detective Lorenzo walks over to the house with the blue shutters and before he could even knock on the door it swings open. An elderly woman in her 70's wearing a purple housecoat with rollers in her hair and purple house shoes and wearing glasses answers and says "hi handsome what can I do for you?"

"Are you Mrs. Marmalade? Well yes, I am."

"I would like to ask you a few questions if that's okay."

"Sure, come on in I just put on a pot of coffee and made some cookies. Are you Shiloh's new boyfriend? "

"We are good friends."

"Oh, I get it friends with benefits huh."

"No ma'am (he laughs) nothing like that."

"I understand you don't want to tell an old lady you barely know, but I see and hear things."

"Yes ma'am, that's why I'm here. I was hoping

you could help me with something."

"Sure, anything for such a handsome young man. You're lucky I'm not 30 years younger. I would give that Shiloh some competition. I sure was a looker back in the day."

"Yes, I'm sure you were and you still are."

"You are so sweet."

"Now Mrs. Marmalade, what can you tell me about the coming and goings of Kitty and Vito's house? Anything no matter how small you may think it is will help tremendously. I'm investigating the disappearance of a woman and anything you can tell me might help a great deal."

"Can you stay for dinner? I made a lovely meatloaf and some roasted potatoes with corn on the cob and a homemade apple pie for dessert or you can have me for dessert instead and she winks at him and smiles. I might remember more on a full stomach."

"Yes ma'am, I would be delighted to stay for dinner."

She sets the table for two and puts wine on the table and lights candles all around the house and on the table and puts on some Frank Sinatra. Mrs.

Marmalade lost her husband to cancer a year

ago. She is still in denial and thinks he is still alive.

"Remember we danced to this song on our wedding night, I remember it like it was yesterday. Let's eat my love."

They eat in silence for a few moments.

"So, what can you tell me about your neighbors?"

"Well, they have a lot of traffic going in and out, and when no one is home at Kitty's house I see strange men and a young lady going into the house. They don't turn on any lights but I see a flashlight going through the house and it looks very suspicious if you ask me. I saw Shiloh and her brother take off in a hurry the other day then right after they left a man started tailing them. I think it was her man friend that is staying with them. Then I saw Vito taking pictures and a very beautiful woman showed up at Vito's. She looked Cuban. I see random cars driving by the house all hours of the night. How about that dessert now? I made your favorite."

"Excuse me! Are you feeling okay Mrs. Marmalade?"

She starts staring out at the stars from the balcony and listening to the music and says, "dance with me, my love." She grabs his hand and starts dancing with him before he could say no. "Oh, how I love Dick so much."

"Mrs. Marmalade, are you sure you are, okay? You just told me you love dick so much."

"Yes, I do with all my heart. I don't know how I am going to live without Dick the rest of my life. He was a great man.:

"Oh, your husband's name was Dick?"

"Yes, what did you think I meant."

"Well I must be going now, you have been a huge help, and thank you for dinner."

Detective Lorenzo goes back over to Kitty's house and she was having a beer and pizza.

"Well, did you find out anything? I'm having beer and pizza. Would you like some?"

"No, I don't think so, so I just spent the last two hours over at crazy Marmalade's house. She fed me dinner and wine by candle light and listened to Frank Sinatra and had me dancing with her. There were times when I think she thought I was her dead husband. The poor woman needs help. I think she was trying to seduce me. I didn't know her husband's name was Dick, and when she told me she couldn't live the rest of her life without dick I didn't know what to say."

Kitty started laughing so hard that tears were coming down her cheeks.

"It's good to see you laughing even if it is at my own expense and he smiles. I think I have enough evidence now that I should be able to find Ginger. I'm still going to have an officer with you around the clock."

"I think I may have misjudged you, detective."

"Well thank you for saying that but just know that I am doing my best and everything is going to work out."

"Thank you."

CHAPTER 17

Ginger wakes up a little disoriented with a chain around her ankle in a small room with a cot, a dirty sink, and a dirty toilet. There's a picture of water sitting on the floor next to the cot with a ham and cheese sandwich and a bowl of grapes on a tray.

There's a small camera in the corner watching her every move.

Ginger takes a look around the room and down at her ankle. "What the hell is going on and where the hell am I? Did I die and go to hell? That's it, I'm in purgatory. No, wait a minute, there's a picture of water sitting here so I don't think I'm in hell because I don't think they have water in hell. Don't panic. That's the worst thing anyone can do his panic and make the situation worse. Maybe this is just a bad dream so if I go back to sleep then I will wake up in my bed with Dillan beside me. How did I get here? Wait, I remember Fiona gave me a drink then I felt sick and needed to lie down and she got someone to give me a ride but that's the last thing I remember. I think she may have drugged me but why I don't get it?" She starts yelling for someone to show their face and tell her what they want with her. No one responds to her; she hears a couple of cars pull up and the doors shut then she hears talking but can't make out what is being said.

"Help, someone, I'm being held against my will. Can you hear me out there?

Please come help me. I'm chained up like a damn dog."

The door opens slowly and someone walks in but their face is all covered so she can't see who is behind the mask.

"What do you want with me?"

"You must eat the food that was brought for you."

"I don't want any damn food, I want answers."

"In due time, in due time. You better hope we get results or you will find yourself at the bottom of the river."

"What results? What are you talking about?"

"You're not making any sense, what do you mean?"

"I mean she better produces results and cooperate. She has the key and we need it. It's vital for us to get it."

"She doesn't have any damn key; she keeps telling you so what makes you think she has it."

"Trust me she has it and if she was any kind of friend to you, she would have told you about it."

"I don't believe you."

"You don't have to believe me but what I'm telling you is a fact. You are our insurance policy that we get what we want and if we don't get what we want, well let's say a lot of people are going to die in the process". He turns around to walk out the door.

"Wait! Can't you unchain me? Where am I going to go? I can't escape, there's no way out."

He ignores her and continues to walk out of the room and locks the door.

Kitty goes back to the club and goes to the locker room to start snooping in Fiona's locker to see if she can find anything to help in the disappearance of Ginger. She finds an address so she puts it in her pocket and continues to look for more clues. The office phone rings so Kitty runs to answer it hoping it might be Ginger.

"Hello?"

The voice on the other end has been altered so it won't be noticeable.

"Is this Kitty?"

"Yes, who is this?"

"I'm your worst nightmare if you don't do as I say. I have your friend here with me and if you don't cooperate, well let's say she will be taking her last breath very soon."

"You better not hurt her; how do I know she is still alive."

"You don't."

"I want to hear her so I know she is okay."

"The man puts the phone up to Ginger's ear, Kitty help me." The man takes the phone away.

"Okay, now you know she is okay, you have 48 hours to get me the key or she dies. I will be in touch to give you the details."

"I don't have any key; how am I supposed to give you what I don't have."

"You better find a way or you both die and the phone disconnects."

"Don't worry Ginger, I'm coming for you. Everything will be okay, I promise."

Kitty straps her pistol to her right inner thigh and straps her switchblade to her left inner thigh and she puts on her utility belt with her stun gun, pepper spray, smoke bombs, and a few grenades. She grabs a machine gun and straps her bullets around her chest and puts on her headband like Rambo. She runs out and jumps on her bike and takes off.

Detective Lorenzo's men are still following her and they called the detective to let him know how she is dressed and that she is all geared up for battle.

"Okay, I'm on my way. Whatever you do, do not lose her. If she knows you are following her, she will do her best to lose you. Stay back but keep her insight."

"Yes Sir."

Detective Lorenzo Pages Kitty, then he pages Shiloh.

"Shiloh calls him back immediately. What's going on Eddie?"

"We have a problem. I have a few men keeping an eye on your mom and it appears she is dressed for battle. I don't know where you are or what you are doing but you need to get back here right away."

"I'm on my way to Washington DC right now."

"It will have to wait; you need to get here now."

"Okay we are on our way. I will book the first flight out."

Shiloh gets off the phone and tells Daryl there has been a change in plans and she explains that they need to get back ASAP, mom needs their help.

Shiloh and Daryl get to the airport but can't get a flight out right away so they get a Mac flight (Military Airlift Command), which will be leaving in about 15 minutes. They arrive in St. Louis and rent a car to take them home. Shiloh calls Detective Lorenzo to let him know that they are home now and want to know where her mom is.

"As of right now she is cruising around the East Side. I paged her at the same time I paged you but she hasn't called me yet."

"Okay, I will page her and find out what she is up to.' Shiloh pages Kitty.

"Kitty calls her right back. Shiloh dear you're back home?"

"Yes mom, where are you? We need to talk, can you come home now?"

"I can't, they have Ginger and I need to go and rescue her."

"Mom it's too dangerous for you to do it alone, come home and let me and Daryl help."

"They are going to kill her Shiloh."

"Then tell me where you are going and we will meet you there."

"I'm not sure exactly, a man called and said for me to produce the key within 48 hours or she dies. So I went to Fiona's locker hoping to find something that will lead me to her and I found this address but I'm not sure where it leads."

"Okay, what is the address you have and we will check it out?"

Kitty gives her the address.

"Okay mom, you need to hang tight and we need to figure out a plan. Don't do anything yet. We are on our way."

"I can't promise anything Shiloh and she hangs up."

"Dammit!"

"What is it, Shiloh?" Daryl asks.

"I told mom to hang tight and we would be on our way, she says she can't promise anything and hangs up the phone. You know what that means, she's going to do her own thing and not wait and get herself into some real trouble. We've got to hurry.

I'm going to call Giovanni and his boys. He said if I needed his help just to holla at him. So I'm going to take him up on that."

"Alright Shiloh, while you do that I've got a few home boys that will help also, so I'm going to give them a call."

Shiloh also called the detective to let him know they are back in town. "We need to talk. I have some very incriminating evidence that I need to turn over to you right away. We were on our way to the FBI when you paged me but we came here instead and people are trying to kill us to get their hands on it." Shiloh explains everything to detective Lorenzo.

"Okay babe, stay put and I'm on my way and I will take care of it."

Lorenzo shows up and Shiloh hands over all the evidence that she had except she didn't tell him about the letter, money, or diamonds.

"I will take this down to the precinct and review it and start getting the arrest warrants in place and contact the FBI. This is huge, it's going to be the arrest of the century. Shiloh, you need to stay put and hang tight until you hear from me, so don't do anything stupid."

"Eddie, man, I can't promise you that, my mom is missing and I need to go and find her before she does something stupid and gets herself hurt or killed. The men you said you have on my mom watching her, have you heard from them? Do they know where she is at or did she give them the slip because you know she is good at giving the slip."

"No, she hasn't given them the slip as of yet but I did warn them that she is like Whodini." (They laugh).

"Well, I've got a few errands to run so hit me up when you get finished."

"I will Shiloh and I mean it don't do anything stupid, wait until you hear from me."

The detective left with the evidence that I gave him so now I need to get on the horn and give Giovanni and his boys a call and incorporate their help in taking these guys down and bringing Mom and Ginger home safely. Daryl is on the phone trying to enlist the help of his homeboys also.

I decided to go downstairs and sit on the porch for a bit when I see this woman walk up and go into uncle Vito's house and she just gives me the evilest look a person can give you so I stare right back at her so she knows that I am not intimidated in the least. Uncle Vito comes out a few minutes later with this woman and his boys.

"Hey uncle Vito, how's everything going I haven't had much time to talk to you lately."

"Yea, I know Shiloh, we will talk soon but I have some stuff to attend to right now." "Okay, I'm going to hold you to that, who's your friend?"

"Lucinda I would like for you to meet my niece, Shiloh."

Lucinda looks her up and down and says something in Spanish and walks off

"It was nice meeting you too Lucinda," Shiloh yells after her.

"I promise we will talk later on when I get back."

CHAPTER 18

"Where are we going to find this Kitty?" Lucinda asks.

"Well, we can start with her club over on the East Side."

They headed over to the club and when they got there, they saw a sign on the door that said (temporarily closed due to unforeseen circumstances, sorry for any inconveniences). They tried all the doors and they all were locked. Lucinda pulls out her gun and shoots off the lock of one of the doors and she proceeds to enter looking in all the rooms and offices but no one is in sight. "Well, it's obvious she is not here." They start trashing the place and turning things upside down and they turn on the gas stoves. Lucinda is outraged and starts shooting holes in the walls and grabs a couple of gas cans and pours gas all over the club then she sets it on fire. As they all walk away from the club it makes an explosion that you can hear for miles. "I want her found and alive."

"We do have the best friend held up down by the river in one of those abandoned buildings."

"Well, why didn't you say that in the first place.

Take me to her. I'm sure this Kitty will be looking for her friend so we will give her a little help in finding her then we will have her right where we want."

Vito shows Lucinda where Ginger is being held so she opens the cell door and walks in and takes one look at Ginger and says "Damn she's like 90 years old did you kidnap her from the nursing home?"

"I beg your pardon; you would look 20 years older too if you were held captive in a nasty place like this for days."

"Where is Kitty?"

"How would I know I've been here against my will. Who are you and what do you want with Kitty?"

"I will be asking the questions here. Where's the key?"

"I'm tired of hearing about some stupid key, I keep telling everyone that there is no key. You're going to be in some hot water when they find me."

"What makes you so sure they are going to find you? You will be down at the bottom of the river where no one will find you. I'll give you this, you are one gutsy old lady." (Lucinda turns and walks out the door).

Kitty starts to snoop around along the riverfront

and she notices some gunmen guarding this abandoned warehouse so she moves in to get a closer look. *This must be where they are holding Ginger. I told you I would come and find you Ginger, just hold on I'm coming. I need a diversion.* She notices some boats down on the dock so she sneaks her way down there without being seen and she cuts the gas lines to where gas is pouring out then she shoots a firebomb at the boats and there's a big explosion. While everyone is running down to the docks to see what is going on Kitty is high tailing it back to the warehouse where it's being guarded by two men. She jumps out at one of the men and points her gun at him and demands him to open the door. He does as he is told when someone comes up behind her and tells her to drop her weapon and he shoves her into the room with Ginger.

"Oh my God, Ginger, thank you Jesus, you're alive I've been looking all over for you. They hug for a long minute now we need to get out of here."

"Kitty look at me. They have me chained like a dog." "Don't you worry about a thing we will get out of here?"

Back at the house Shiloh and Daryl both heard

the explosions and they could see all this black smoke coming from across the river so they jumped in Shiloh's car with Cochise and Nikita right along with them and they headed over to the East Side. "I've got a bad feeling Daryl, let's go check out the club first. " When they get to the club, they see it all up in flames and firefighters trying to put it out. There is nothing that they can do so Daryl goes and meets his boys and Shiloh went to meet Giovani.

Lucinda walks back in the room where Ginger and Kitty were being held. "Well, Well, Well look what we have here a female version of Rambo." (She laughs).

"Kitty spits on her."

Lucinda takes the butt of her gun and hits her in the face. She points the gun at her head and says "Now you are going to tell me where the key is before I blow you brains all over the place."

"You want the key to my house well why didn't you just say that. Here it is now can we go."

"You think you're funny?" Just when Lucinda was getting ready to pull the trigger the door bursts open.

"Thank God Dillan, you found us, now you're in

big trouble lady the calvary is here."

Lucinda laughs. 'Are you sure about that?" She walks over to Dillian, gives him a long kiss and he kisses her back.

"What is she talking about Dillian?"

"I'm sorry babe but this is the way it has to be. I can't go to prison. Do you know what they do to guys like me in prison? I've put away most of them and I wouldn't last one day there."

"Dillian, I can't believe you played me like that. I thought you loved me. What happened to you? I know you, you're not a bad person. We can figure this out together".

"I know I've hurt you and I'm sorry but now I can't let you out alive. "He unchains her ankle.

"So what is your plan now Dillian? Are you going to shoot us?"

"No, I'm not going to shoot you, but I'm afraid I'm going to have to tie you up and gag you and put you in the freight carrier and drop you at the bottom of the river."

"So this was just all an act to try and find some key that doesn't exist! I hope it was worth it to you. You won't get away with it Dillian."

"Get rid of them," Lucinda says as she walks out of the room.

"Who the hell is that woman?" Kitty asks.

"That is Lucinda also known as the black widow, she is very powerful and is part of one of the biggest cartels in Mexico. She is not one to be messed with, she is very dangerous and you don't want to cross her.'

"So you're her puppet."

"I'm nobody's puppet, do you hear me."

"Of course I hear you, you are right in front of me, how can I not hear you, I'm old not deaf."

Dillan grabs her and gives her one last kiss and she bites his lip drawing blood so he hits her so hard that he knocks her unconscious. Kitty screams at him. He ignores her screams and gags Ginger and ties her up then puts her in a crate and two goons come in to move her.

"Where are you taking her?" Kitty demands to know.

The men didn't respond to Kitty but just carried off Ginger with Dillian right behind them. He looks over his shoulder at Kitty and says they will be back for her.

Daryl and his crew got a hold of a couple of helicopters and started flying overhead to see what they could find when they saw a couple of armed guys standing guard outside an abandoned building. They started firing their guns at them so they took cover and fired back. The guys that took Ginger are on a boat so they can drop her at the bottom of the river. Giovani and his boys are all suited up and on the ground searching all the warehouses. Shiloh is checking out the other boats down on the dock that didn't go up in flames. Someone comes up behind Shiloh and tells her to turn around.

"I want you to see it coming when I shoot you".

Shiloh turns around," Fiona! Why are you doing this? It's not too late to turn yourself in. We can help you."

"You don't have any idea who I am do you?"

"Why don't you tell me."

"You took my father away from me when I was just 9 years old. Do you know what that does to a child? They put me in a foster home after foster home with these awful people that call themselves parents. They drank a lot and abused us so I ran away when I was 15 and I swore I would find you and make you pay for taking away my father."

'Your father was a very terrible person and did some really terrible things to people. He deserved to go to prison."

"No, I don't believe you. I needed my father in my life and now I have him back and we can now be a family and I'm not going to let you or anyone else ruin that for me."

"Listen to me Fiona, please. I don't want to hurt you but you have to believe what I'm saying is true."

Fiona laughs. "You hurt me, I'm the one with the gun."

I'm sorry Fiona and Shiloh dropped a knife out of her sleeve into her hand and threw it at her hand where the gun is and she dropped the gun then Fiona lunged at her and Shiloh moved. Fiona fell on her face then jumped up and went after Shiloh again. They both fell to the ground wrestling and Shiloh manages to pull her pistol out of her boot they both fought over the gun and it went off, blood is going everywhere. Shiloh gets up and Fiona is lying lifeless on the ground. Shiloh takes off in one of the boats and goes after the men on the other boat. They start shooting at Shiloh and she shoots back. She hit one of the men and he fell overboard. She continues chasing the other guy and she catches up to him and rams him in the side making him lose control for a minute. She stands on the bow of her boat and jumps onto the other boat. She didn't make it all the way but managed to grab a hold of the stern and pulled herself up to get on board.

The guy turns around, "Jack" or should I say captain?

"Well, it's been a long time. I've been waiting for this moment when we would finally meet face to face again." He grabs a long pipe and swings it at Shiloh but she ducks and he misses. She gives him a roundhouse kick to the head and knocks him back a few feet. He gains his composure and grabs a chain and hits her with it and knocks her down then he jumps on her and puts his hands around her throat and starts to choke her, she kicks her knee up into his groin and he releases her neck then she gets up and kicks him in the knee bringing him down and she grabs him by the hair and bangs his head on the edge of the boat. He takes his elbow and punches her in the side of the face then Shiloh grabs her stun gun and zapps him and he falls backward over the side of the boat. Shiloh jumps up in the seat and steers the boat barely missing the barge coming down the river. Once she gets it under control, she gets a crowbar to pry open the crate where Ginger is and helps her out.

Detective Lorenzo pulls up beside them in a Coast Guard Boat and helps Ginger onboard and Shiloh tells him about the other two men in the river so they go to pick them up.

Shiloh takes the boat and goes back to shore so she can find her mom.

Giovani and his men found the warehouse where they are keeping Kitty. They go in with blazing guns and shooting. They threw in a smoke bomb in one of the buildings and the men came running out coughing and choking.

Daryl goes into one of the warehouses and sees a locked door and shoots off the lock.

"Daryl you're here." Kitty runs over to hug him. "We have to go save Ginger, they put her into a crate and are going to dump her at the bottom of the river."

"Mom, it's okay now you and Ginger are both safe now. Ginger is on her way to the hospital and the guys that had her are in custody now. Stay behind me and I will get you out of here". They leave the warehouse and Daryl puts Kitty in a safe spot and tells her to stay put and this will be over very shortly. Giovani and his men are throwing smoke bombs in all the warehouse buildings to smoke everyone out.

Vito comes running out of one of the buildings and he says, “Giovani what are you doing here?”

“Well, if it isn’t cousin Vito. I made a promise that I would always be there for Shiloh no matter what and I intend to keep that promise. You had better get out of here before they come and get you too. I’m not going to put my cousin behind bars but I will stop you from hurting Shiloh or her mom. I think you better leave now and never look back.”

“I will and thank you Giovani.”

Giovani continues smoking out all the warehouses and throwing a few grenades in them and blowing them up.

Shiloh catches up with Giovani and says, “Thanks for your help “G” but you guys better go now because the cops and feds are on their way. Thanks for everything.”

“Anytime you need me just give me a call, I will always be there.” Giovani and his boys pull out before the cops arrive.

Vito and Lucinda take off and go back to the house to pack up and get out of town. He calls ahead to the airport for them to have his jet-fueled up and ready to go when they get there.

Nikita and Cochise are in one of the warehouses where the drugs and money are at and have two men cornered until the cops come in.

Daryl and Shiloh take off to go find Vito and the black widow. They go back to the house and see that they left in a hurry and they remember that Vito has a jet at the airport so they head out to the airport to cut them off at the pass. Shiloh calls the detective to let him know what is going on so the detective calls the airport and tells them that all flights are grounded until further notice.

Daryl and Shiloh pull up at the airport and see the jet trying to take off so they drive their car onto the airfield and Daryl manages to jump on one of the wings and pulls himself into the cargo area to get on board. The jet pulls up and takes off into the air. Daryl sneaks his way up into the jet and grabs Lucinda from behind and puts her in a sleeper hold and she is out. He goes into the cockpit to where Vito and the pilot are. “Hey, Uncle Vito are you going somewhere?”

"Daryl, how did you get on board?"

"Don't mind that, you need to turn this jet around and land back at the airport right now."

"I'm sorry Daryl but we can't do that. What did you do with Lucinda?"

"Don't worry about her, she is taking a little nap. I need you to put this thing on automatic pilot." The pilot did as he was told, then the two men were instructed to go to the back of the jet where he gagged them and tied them up. He then went to the cockpit and turned the jet around and landed it back at the airport where the police were waiting for their arrival. The FBI came aboard and escorted them off and into the back of their car.

"Well, thanks to you guys we now have the biggest drug cartel behind bars."

Shiloh walks up to the car where they have her uncle Vito and she just looks at him and says, "how could you do this uncle Vito, I trusted you and I loved you and you betrayed me."

"I was never going to hurt you Shiloh and I do love you with all my heart." "You might not hurt me but hurting my mom is the same thing as hurting me."

"I'm sorry Shiloh, I never meant to hurt you, I

only hope someday you can find it in your heart to forgive me."

"Ma'am we need to be going now." Says one of the FBI men.

Daryl hugs Shiloh and they get into their car and head to the hospital where Ginger and Kitty are at.

Detective Lorenzo is at the hospital waiting for Shiloh to show up. Shiloh runs up to him and hugs him, how's mom and Ginger?

"They will be okay, how are you doing?"

"I'm okay, just glad this is all over and behind us now so we can all rest easy and get on with our lives."

"Well, we have enough evidence to put these guys away for life. I have someone here that wants to see you."

"Ace walks in with his FBI jacket on."

"What is this?" Asks Shiloh.

"I'm sorry I couldn't tell you Shiloh but I was undercover and had to bring these guys down and I knew they were coming for your mom."

"You could have told me the truth, since when do we keep secrets from each other? I thought we could trust one another."

"We can Shiloh and I meant what I said. I do love you and want to spend the rest of my life with you."

"No, I'm sorry Ace that just isn't possible." (She turns and walks out the door).

Shiloh turns to Eddie and tells him she needs to be by herself for a while to figure things out. Kitty and Ginger were released from the hospital and Shiloh and Daryl took them home.

Shiloh turns to her mom and says, "I have to tell you something. Your club was burned to the ground. I'm so sorry."

"That's okay honey, I had a really good insurance policy so it will pay out pretty good then we can find somewhere else to move to and start over."

When they all got back home and went upstairs, they saw Macc at the top of the stairs waiting for them.

Kitty says, "Macc you should be behind bars with the rest of the clan."

"Miss Kitty it's not what you think. I had nothing to do with any of that mess, I was fresh out of prison and needed to make some money so I could get back on my feet and get on with my life and start over and go straight. When Shiloh hired me that's when I started thinking that I needed to help her and be on the right side of the law for once."

Kitty called the police to have them come and take him way.

"No! Mom he is right, he could have easily helped uncle Vito instead but he stayed loyal to me so I can't turn him in." Shiloh hands him $10,000 and tells him to take care of himself and he needs to go before the police show up downstairs.

"Thank you, Miss Shiloh, I will always remember you and your kindness." He takes off out the back way so he won't be seen.

Detective Lorenzo and his team show up at Vito's and confiscate all his equipment and paraphernalia.

Kitty walks down the back stairs to Vito's and she sees Tiny in handcuffs.

"What's going on here? Why is Tiny in cuffs?"

"I'm sorry Ma'am but you can't be here?"

"Like hell, I can't, I own this place."

Eddie walks in and tells her to have a seat.

"NO! I think I will stand. I demand to know what

the hell is going on here".

"Okay, Tiny was paid off to keep an eye on you and get information from you.

He is willing to testify against them for immunity."

"Tiny, is this true? Please tell me it's not true. What was all this talk about you loving me and wanting to be with me forever? That was all a lie also."

"I do love you Kitty and I meant every word I said. I did it for us so we could have a better life. It was all for you. I wouldn't let anyone hurt you. I figured I would get the money and we could go away somewhere. You have to believe me."

"I don't have to believe anything. We didn't need the money; I had enough money. Well, this is it Tiny don't ever come looking for me again. You betrayed me and I can never forgive you for that."

Eddie puts him in the back of the squad car and they drive off.

CHAPTER 19

18 MONTHS LATER

Kitty and Ginger are on the beach somewhere in Florida sipping on Margaritas and enjoying the sun watching the view of all the young studs running around half-naked. Shiloh is watching her twin girls Crystal and Ashley playing in the sand.

Daryl just got out of therapy to help him deal with everything that happened in Vietnam and he still sees someone once a week to help him cope.

“Man, this is the life girls, we should have done this sooner,” Kitty says.

Eddie walks up behind Shiloh and hugs her and grabs her hand then they take a stroll on the beach while grandma watches the twins.

Made in United States
Orlando, FL
02 January 2023